Show Time for a Showdown

Holding out his left hand as if to keep the younger man at a distance, Clint knew better than to waste his breath with any more appeals to some nonexistent rational side. Instead, he gave a simple word of warning.

"Don't."

Whether or not he was affected by the word, Anderson stopped less than ten feet away from Clint and planted his feet in the sandy soil. He squared his shoulders and fixed his target with an intense gaze.

For the next few seconds, all Clint could hear was the wind churning down the street and Maria's feet shuffling on the other side of the saloon's front door. She must have tipped the others inside about what was going on, because all of the chatter and commotion within the saloon had come to a halt.

It seemed as though the only two living creatures on the face of the earth were Clint and Anderson. In the space of a few seconds, both men knew that number was about to go down by one . . .

DON'T MISS THESE
ALL-ACTION WESTERN SERIES
FROM THE BERKLEY PUBLISHING GROUP

THE GUNSMITH by J. R. Roberts
Clint Adams was a legend among lawmen, outlaws, and ladies. They called him . . . the Gunsmith.

LONGARM by Tabor Evans
The popular long-running series about Deputy U.S. Marshal Long—his life, his loves, his fight for justice.

SLOCUM by Jake Logan
Today's longest-running action Western. John Slocum rides a deadly trail of hot blood and cold steel.

BUSHWHACKERS by B. J. Lanagan
An action-packed series by the creators of Longarm! The rousing adventures of the most brutal gang of cutthroats ever assembled—Quantrill's Raiders.

DIAMONDBACK by Guy Brewer
Dex Yancy is Diamondback, a Southern gentleman turned con man when his brother cheats him out of the family fortune. Ladies love him. Gamblers hate him. But nobody pulls one over on Dex . . .

WILDGUN by Jack Hanson
Will Barlow's continuing search for his daughter, kidnapped by the Blackfeet Indians who slaughtered the rest of his family.

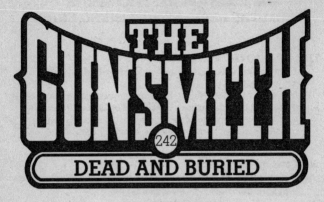

DEAD AND BURIED

J. R. ROBERTS

JOVE BOOKS, NEW YORK

This is a work of fiction. Names, characters, places, and incidents either are the product of the author's imagination or are used fictitiously, and any resemblance to actual persons, living or dead, business establishments, events, or locales is entirely coincidental.

DEAD AND BURIED

A Jove Book / published by arrangement with
the author

PRINTING HISTORY
Jove edition / February 2002

Visit our website at
www.penguinputnam.com

ISBN: 0-515-13253-5

A JOVE BOOK®
Jove Books are published by The Berkley Publishing Group,
a division of Penguin Putnam Inc.,
375 Hudson Street, New York, New York 10014.
JOVE and the "J" design
are trademarks belonging to Penguin Putnam Inc.

PRINTED IN THE UNITED STATES OF AMERICA

10 9 8 7 6 5 4 3 2 1

ONE

When Eldon Greary first staked his claim at the base of the Grand Wash Cliffs in Arizona, he thought the land he'd chosen must have been haunted. How else could he explain all of the pieces of equipment that went missing or the strange sounds he heard in the darkest hours of the night? What else could account for the strange feelings that would plague him during the day, making him swear that he was being watched?

Raised in a superstitious family who threw nearly as much salt over their shoulders as they did onto their food, Eldon didn't think it peculiar in the least that ghosts or demons might be troubling him. After all, such things happened to most people and they didn't even know it.

Back in the old country where his family had come from, the Little People were just another part of the locals' common sense. Of course they existed. Denying such a fact was just as idiotic as denying the number of fingers at the end of your hands or spitting into the face of the Good Lord himself.

Healthy people just didn't test their luck like that. Not if they wanted to stay healthy, anyway.

Spending most of his fifty-eight years sifting through the dirt and chipping away inside the guts of mountains only strengthened his belief in such things. After all, what else but luck could explain why one man could pull a chunk of gold from the bottom of the same river that didn't give anything to the rest of the prospectors but silt and wet pans?

Luck was a big part of a miner's life. Fate, jinxes, curses, blessings, Eldon Greary believed in it all. Just because he couldn't see any of it didn't make it any less real in his eyes. He went to church and talked to God the same way he pleaded to the spirits of the river when he shook his tin plate back and forth in the slow current. He sang to the Holy Ghost just the same from a pew or from a cold dark shaft that might collapse on top of him at any moment.

Belief was never in short supply within Eldon Greary's heart. The only regret he had was that such things weren't so easily handed over from one generation to the next.

As much as he loved his daughter, Eldon was never able to do much more than scare the poor little thing with the ghost stories he would tell. Maybe it was because she was born and raised in America, where there just wasn't as much of the pure spirits running through the ground and flying through the air.

Youth was like that, though. Whether it was a young person or a young country, those without the benefit of perspective were clean and pure. Eldon's little girl, just like the country that had become their home, was untouched by most of what Eldon had grown up with. That purity was what he loved about America. He loved the country enough to pack up and sail away from his home and raise his only child there. But when the purity of the land combined with the purity of her mind, Jillian became very doubtful concerning things like luck and spirits.

Religion was one thing, but for her the rest was just stories.

Still, Jillian was the light of Eldon's life. As a child, she'd been the one constant joy in his existence and as an adult, his single best friend. She'd traveled with him across the country and was the one person who believed in every plan that entered his mind. She hadn't even complained about pulling up the roots they'd sunk for themselves in northern Colorado. Once they'd arrived in Arizona, she'd simply gotten her bearings, took a look around and planted new roots.

Eldon loved her for that, which made it all the more difficult to admit the incredible danger that he'd put them both in.

As soon as he'd heard the first nightly rumblings and noticed the first missing items, he should have known better than to tempt the spirits by sticking around where he so obviously wasn't wanted.

But it was too late now. Even if there were no ghosts against him, Eldon knew his luck was bad and every time he even thought about leaving, things just seemed to get worse. In fact, just the other week, Eldon was packing up his things when Jillian came running back to their cabin with tears streaming down her face.

Someone had tried to attack her on the way into town. No doubt, those thugs were pushed by the spirits to go after his little girl for what he'd been getting ready to do. They'd wanted him to leave before, but now all they wanted was for him to sit and take his punishment like a man.

Maybe then they would leave him alone. Maybe then, they would let his daughter live out her days in peace. The very notion that he might have called down such bad luck was nearly enough to bring a tear to Eldon's eye.

How could he be so stupid?

How could he be so thoughtless?

"Daddy?" The voice came from behind the rocker that Eldon had put on his front porch.

Quickly swiping at his face, Eldon turned around to see his daughter standing in the front doorway. She looked like an angel, reminding him of her dearly departed mother. Even after a life spent in the outdoors, her skin was still pale and smooth. The slight upward turn of her nose came from his side of the family, however, but on her it looked so much cuter than the pug snout sitting in the middle of Eldon's face.

Jillian's hair was long and thick, forming a natural flow of tight, curly waves that was usually kept tied back behind her head by a simple black ribbon. She looked at him now, her hazel eyes looking more brown than green at the moment, with a concerned expression on her face.

"What's the matter?" she asked.

Eldon grabbed hold of the worn arms of the rocker and pushed himself out and up to his feet. "Just watching the sunset, is all," he replied. "I was gonna fix myself a pipe and then get to bed. Big day tomorrow."

The air was beginning to lose the warm blessing of the sun. Jillian stepped outside and wiped her hands on the front of her apron, pulling the material away from her waist. The dress she wore was a plain blue-and-white checked design, which she'd sewn herself. That skill, along with many others, was something that she'd learned on her own as a way to make their lives easier and more self-sufficient. Besides stitching and mending, she was a gardener and one hell of a cook.

"You thinking about that mine again?" she asked, even though she knew well enough that he wasn't.

Ever since those men had given her trouble, Jillian could sense the difference in her father's face, his tone, even his posture. He was a guarded man now, always keeping his eye on everyone else. Never allowing himself to let his defenses down even for a minute.

"Yeah," he said, just like she knew he would. "The mine."

"Well stewing about it isn't going to cut through any rock. Why don't you just come inside and have some of that pie I made today? I left it out on the sill this afternoon and it was still there without so much as a nibble taken off of it. I was beginning to think you might have gotten lost in a tunnel or something."

Eldon chuckled a bit, but the smile on his face was clearly straining his muscles. "I'll be there in a minute," he said while fishing the old, chewed pipe from his shirt pocket. "How about brewing me some coffee to go along with that pie?"

Smiling, Jillian reached out and stroked the gristly beard that had covered her father's face for as long as she could remember. Although the rest of his hair had begun to silver and thin out, the man's features were still the same. The wide-set, brown eyes. The bulbous, upturned nose. Even the coarse texture of his skin remained as it was for all of her twenty-three years.

She gave him a hug and pat him on the shoulder. "Well, try not to stay out too much longer. I don't want you catching cold."

Jillian stepped back inside and busied herself with preparing dessert. More than anything, she wished she could keep her father from finding out about what was headed their way. Once he knew, the weariness in his eyes would only get worse and the smile on his face would become more tarnished.

Then again, the sooner he found out about it, the sooner they could deal with the problem. For right now, however, there wasn't much either of them could do besides enjoy the cool night air.

Eldon looked out at the desolate horizon. He'd built the cabin facing the mountains rather than the nearby town so he could look out at what he loved the most. Inside those mountains was hope. Deep, deep inside.

TWO

After spending so much of the last year up north, Clint Adams had ridden down into the southwest merely to escape the cold and snow that had chilled him to the bone for most of this past winter. Lately, though, he'd gotten used to the dry warmth of the air during the day and the cool tranquillity of the desert night. Even Eclipse seemed to have taken to the change in climate and terrain, running with carefree abandon whenever Clint so much as flicked the reins.

He knew the gambling circuit was a major source of income for many of the towns in the area, which gave Clint even more reason to slow down and take his time while passing through the area. Eventually, he was going to head back into West Texas and check in on the closest place he'd called home for some time.

It had been a while since he'd been to Labyrinth and the thought of cooling his heels in such a familiar place seemed especially attractive. Clint even felt a pang of homesickness when he tried to think about just how long it had been since he'd seen that town or any of his friends who lived there.

But then he would always shake the wistfulness from his head and look up at whatever sky was currently over his head. With the sun well on its way to setting, the clouds had become crimson smudges thrown onto the great heavenly canvas. At this time of the day, even the wind seemed to take a few moments to stop what it was doing and give a moment of silence in honor to the wondrous display overhead.

Eclipse trod over the sand-covered rock at a leisurely pace. The Darley Arabian stallion flicked its tail at the occasional insect and twitched his ears at the rare sound, but other than that, he seemed to be enjoying himself every bit as much as the man upon his back.

A pack of coyotes cried out in the distance, causing both man and horse to look in the direction of the sound. It was then that Clint saw a few buildings huddled close together no more than a few miles away. The sloping rocks and nearby mountain range had hidden the place from view until this moment.

"What do you say, boy?" Clint asked while shifting the reins in his hand. "Should we head for town or spend another night next to a campfire?"

The stallion shook his head and huffed a breath out of his nostrils.

Clint smiled and pated the animal's neck. "I'd have to agree with you. This looks like it's going to be too nice of a night to spend cooped up inside."

He steered Eclipse toward a group of boulders. Once he was there, Clint hopped down from the saddle and formed a circle of smaller rocks. By the looks of it, this was a popular spot for campsites and some of the previous tenants had been kind enough to leave some of their trash behind. The broken wooden crate and burlap sack made excellent kindling, and by the time darkness came, there was a fire roaring high enough to warm Clint's hands as well as his plate of beans.

He sat near his fire, eating a meal that wasn't even close to something he might get at a downright bad restaurant, and enjoyed every last second of it. The stars spread out over him, shining down with such clarity that it was almost frightening to behold. If he looked at it long enough, Clint felt as though he might just fly off the surface of the world and go hurtling into space.

Instead of worrying about that, however, he sifted through his bags for some coffee and set about brewing a pot before drifting off to sleep. The grounds were barely wet by the time he heard a rumbling sound coming from the north. At first, he thought there might be a storm on the way. But then he listened a bit harder and realized that what he'd heard hadn't been thunder.

It was the sound of horses coming his way . . . and fast.

There weren't many of them, but with the open trail in front of him and a wall of mountains not far behind, the sound had been bounced around and amplified enough to give a bad first impression. Clint couldn't see much beyond the faint glimmer of his fire, but he knew that whoever was riding toward him could see the flickering flames better than anything else for miles around.

Although there was no reason to expect trouble, Clint knew better than to put too much faith in things turning out for the best, so just to be on the safe side, he removed the leather thong that held his Colt firmly inside his holster. There was a rifle strapped to his saddle, but since there couldn't have been more than three of four riders at the most, Clint figured the six bullets inside his Colt would do just fine if push came to shove.

Still working on his coffee, Clint positioned himself so that his back was against one of the bigger rocks and waited for his guests to arrive.

As the horses drew closer, they began to slow down. The first thing Clint could see was a vague group of shadowy outlines looming closer and closer with every passing second. The figures fanned out into a half-circle before coming to a stop at the outermost edge of the firelight.

There were four of them, and the next thing Clint saw was the glint of metal in two of the men's hands.

"Evening, gentlemen," Clint said casually. "Care for a cup of coffee?"

"Thanks, but no," one of the riders said just before the click of a hammer being cocked snapped through the air. "We'll have plenty of time for drinks after we bury your ass in this here desert."

THREE

The one doing the talking sat on top of a horse that was so dark it was nothing more than a massive shape in the darkness. The men to either side of him were holding their weapons out in plain sight. Clint strained his ears for any trace of steps coming up from behind, but as far as he could tell, the other men hadn't bothered taking the time to flank him. After all, the fact that they outnumbered him four to one seemed to be enough of an advantage in their eyes.

Clint moved his hands slowly until he had both palms against the rock behind him. "Now just a minute here," he said while pushing himself up to his feet. "There's no need for anyone to get buried anywhere. I don't even know you fellas."

"You don't have to know us, mister. We know you well enough, and that's all that matters. Now, if you tell us what we need to know, I can make sure you die fast or slow."

"I'm not sure I like those choices."

"That's too bad, 'cause they're all you got."

Clint painted a look of fear across his face while he silently figured the odds in his head. From what he could see, the men with the guns were ready to pull their triggers and had already taken aim. The fact that they hadn't sent at least one of their number to come up behind him told Clint that they weren't true professionals. On the other hand, common thieves wouldn't be bothering with all this talk, either.

That made these men something of a mystery in Clint's mind. That, more than anything else, saved their lives.

Clint stood with his left hand out to the side and his right hanging close to his Colt. Using the flickering shadows and weak light thrown off by the fire to his advantage, he moved his gun hand even closer. Either the men hadn't noticed what he was doing, or they were too confident in their numbers to care.

"All right then," Clint said. "What is it you want to know?"

The group's apparent leader brought his horse a little closer to the fire, leaning down so he could glare directly into Clint's eyes when he said, "How many more of you did that old fool pay for?"

"Who are you talking about?"

"Don't start this shit with me," the leader said as his expression twisted into an angry scowl. "The miner. How many men did he hire to fight for him?"

Clint didn't even try to hide the smile as it slipped onto his face. Suddenly, he realized just how far away from professionals these men truly were.

"What's so damn funny?" the first horseman asked.

Raising his hands to chest level, Clint replied, "It's not so much funny as it is—well, actually, it's pretty funny now that I think about it."

For a moment, every one of the horsemen seemed genuinely taken aback by Clint's reaction. Even the ones who were shrouded mostly in darkness seemed to be turning toward their leader as though they honestly didn't know what to do about the crazy man they'd just cornered. The leader didn't have to look toward his men to know what they were thinking. Instead, he swung down off his horse and took a few steps closer to the fire.

Careful not to step too close, the first horseman positioned himself so that he could stare directly across into Clint's eyes without getting in his men's line of fire. He wore the black suit and hat of a gambler, complete with a long dress coat and string tie. Without the horse beneath him, he seemed much shorter than Clint would have even guessed. His light brown hair was clipped close to his scalp, framing a narrow, bony face. "How much is he paying you?"

"Actually," Clint said, "that's the funny part. I still don't have the faintest idea who you're talking about." At that moment, the smile vanished from Clint's face quicker than a bird that had been flushed from the bushes. His eyes turned into intense slits that soaked up the light from the fire and reflected the flames back at each of the horsemen in turn. When he spoke, his voice was cold and sharpened to a fine, steely edge. "So if you boys want to make the single worst decision of your lives, go ahead and start shooting. Otherwise, get the hell away from my camp."

The leader of the horsemen began to go for his weapon, but then got a sudden chill that raked all down his spine when he tried to stare down the man in front of him. Clint glared back without a hint of bravado or menace. All the gunman saw in those eyes was the deadly promise of swift retribution if he was crossed.

For a second, the gunmen looked as though they might step back and leave Clint to his fire and coffee. Then, common sense faded away to be replaced with foolish pride.

"All right then," the leader said. "Have it your way." The man turned to his men and nodded. "Shoot him. Then dig a hole and toss his carcass—"

The rest of his sentence was choked off as soon as he turned around to find the barrel of Clint's pistol less than an inch away from his face. He hadn't heard so much as a hint of movement from the solitary figure. In fact, judging by the look of surprise on his men's faces, none of them had seen Clint move enough to even concern themselves with him.

There had been no more threats or warning. One instant the man was in control of the situation and the next, he was wondering what it would be like when he died.

Clint let the moment sink in on all of the horsemen for a second or two before doing anything else. Drawing the Colt had been as simple and natural to him as drawing a breath. Since he didn't even have to thumb back the hammer of his modified pistol, he'd been able to turn the tables on his would-be attackers without creating more than the subtle noise of metal brushing against leather.

"Since you're so fond of questions," Clint said, "how about answering some of mine? Just who the hell are you and why would you draw on somebody minding his own business in the middle of the desert?"

"Name's Max Hardam," the leader said. "Me and my men are just working to protect our interests, is all. As for the rest . . . you know damn well why we're after you. The old man wouldn't be paying so much if you were taking on an easy job."

Clint could feel the anger raising up inside of him and it must have showed upon his face since all four of the others tensed in anticipation. "Are you so stupid that you *still* can't figure out that I don't know what you're talking about? Who's this old man and what job is he offering?"

Hardam's eyes narrowed and he tilted his head like a confused dog. "You mean you really don't know?"

Clint tensed his arm, pressing the gun's barrel that much closer to Hardam's forehead. "You're testing my patience."

"All right," Hardam said while slowly lifting his hands into the air. "You convinced me. Maybe I made a mistake." Without turning away from Clint, he motioned toward the men behind him who reluctantly lowered their weapons. Hardam then backed away from the fire and climbed into his saddle. Once he was once again looking down on Clint, he added, "But I'll still keep an eye on you just the same. That is, unless you do the smart thing and put this town behind you."

Watching until the sound of the horses had blended in with the rest of the desert's noises, Clint walked around the rocks just to make sure he was truly alone. As far as he could tell, Hardam had taken all of his men with him but that somehow didn't make Clint feel any better.

The coffee was just about ready. After he'd had a chance to drink it down, he packed up and headed for the nearby town. Mostly, that was because he sure as hell didn't feel safe sleeping out in the open knowing that someone like Hardam would be waiting for an opportunity to get the drop on him. Also, there was that little hell-raising part of Clint's brain that simply enjoyed the prospect of pissing the horseman off by going exactly where he'd been forbidden to go.

Normally, Clint preferred riding when he could see a bit more than five feet in front of him, but that very reason was why he wanted to get out of the open and into the relative safety of town. Once he'd moved on and put this area behind him, he would have plenty of time to sleep under the stars. Until then, however, he decided to make the best of it and see what this place had to offer.

By the looks of the dreary little group of dusty buildings huddled together, this town wasn't going to be much more exciting than a circle of rocks. Clint smiled as the phrase "famous last words" sprung instantly to mind.

FOUR

Max Hardam watched from a spot in the darkness that was close enough for him to keep track of the stranger that they'd found camped in the desert, while keeping far enough away to remain out of the other man's sight. With his three men backing him up, Hardam was far from scared of the stranger. After all, it didn't matter how fast a man was on the draw, only a select few were good enough to hit much of anything when the lead started to fly. Hardam knew that much from personal experience.

The four riders sat in the cool night atop horses that knew better than to make so much as a sound as they waited for their commands. Keeping perfectly still except for the occasional twitch of an ear or tail, the group blended in perfectly with the sand and shadows.

Just as Hardam had expected, the stranger packed up his camp and turned toward town, riding for the safety of the nearby buildings. It wouldn't help him, though, since finding a stranger in town was about as hard as finding a shovel in a haystack.

"Should we get after him?" asked the man to Hardam's left.

Jed Bosner was the only one of the three that could have gotten away with breaking the silence before getting the okay from Hardam. Bosner had been with him since they'd both been shit-disturbing kids and even though Hardam had taken the lead of the group, Bosner was given more leniency than any of the others.

Even when they were both in the saddle, Bosner rose nearly three inches over Hardam's head. The dark-skinned, thick-boned man was more imposing on his own two feet, where he towered close to a foot over just about anyone else. His dark, brooding eyes seemed set far back into his skull where they peered out like a pair of snakes hidden beneath the ledge of his brow. The darkness clung to his coal-black hair like tar that ran all the way down to the middle of his back.

"There's no need to follow him," Hardam replied. "Any fool can see where he's goin'. I'd rather let him think he's getting there alone so we can see what he does from there."

Bosner squinted into the shadows until the stranger's horse was swallowed up by the night. "You think he's workin' for the old man?"

"I'm not so sure. Did you see how fast he was on the draw?"

"Yeah. Can't say as I've ever seen anything like it before, though."

"I know. A man like that would be awful expensive to put on a payroll. Much more expensive than someone like old man Greary could afford, that's for damn sure."

"Unless he's been holding out on us."

Hardam considered that for a few seconds and then shook his head. "Nah. If he had that much to spend, Greary would've packed up and taken off by now. Besides, he ain't that good of a liar."

The other two riders sat in silence behind Hardam and Bosner. They were only too glad to follow orders rather than question them since so far that strategy had led to them becoming two of the richest men in town. Of the entire group, Danny Welles was the oldest. He'd handed over his childhood to the U.S. Cavalry and in return got a head full of bad memories and the twin .44 caliber pistols strapped to his waist. The scars on his face were living testament to the Indians he'd been forced to kill in the line of duty when he was a kid. Since the government had turned him into an exterminator of men, he'd decided to go somewhere he could get some real money for it. As for all the blood on his hands . . . that was something he'd learned to live with over the years.

Jon Anderson was the youngest member of the group and had taken to Hardam as a kind of teacher. While the kid didn't carry out his orders with the regimented obedience as displayed by Welles, he was a good student nonetheless and absorbed Hardam's tactics along with Bosner's ruthlessness and Welles's knack for snuffing out his emotions whenever they started to get in the way.

As far as gunmen went, Anderson was a good prospect. As for his position in the gang, he was the first man to be sent into a gunfight and the one in charge of laying down the cover fire upon an escape. The cavalry had taught Welles a name for such a man.

Cannon fodder.

Once the stranger's horse was given a good enough head start, Hardam looked over his shoulder at the other two and signaled for them to get moving. They rode into town only a few minutes after losing sight of the stranger and came to a stop in front of the general store, which was the first building at the edge of town.

"Welles," Hardam said. "I want you and the kid to check the livery and Miss Tammy's place. See if you can find out anything about him or why he's here. Me and Bosner will go to the hotel. Meet us there in a few minutes after you've done what I told you."

Welles was used to baby-sitting detail. He spoke before the kid had a chance to complain about being sent to the stables and asked, "What should we do if we find him?"

"Take him alive if possible," Bosner said. "As long as you don't go in shooting, you should be able to keep him talking long enough for us to find you and back you up."

"What makes you think he won't shoot at us first?" Anderson said.

Hardam shook his head without taking his eyes from the rest of the town. "He won't. If he was that kind, I wouldn't be alive right now. He'll talk to you," he said as he scanned the darkened buildings with a hunter's gaze. "And if he doesn't say what we want to hear, we'll blow his tongue out the back of his head. That one's a loose end and, hired gun or not, we don't need loose ends messing us up when we're so close."

"And if the old man did hire him?" This time it was Bosner who was asking the question. "Then what?"

"Then we hurt him," Hardam replied with an icy tone in his voice. "Hurt all of them so bad that the old man will hand over the mine and all of his gold just to make the hurting stop."

FIVE

Even after Clint found the only saloon in town, he still didn't know exactly where he was. Besides knowing that he was in the northwest section of Arizona near a range of mountains, he didn't know much else. The name of the town might have been written across every building he'd passed, but the darkness was so complete that he felt lucky to see the buildings at all before riding Eclipse directly into one of them.

The Darley Arabian was getting tired and sluggish in his steps, but Clint didn't have much choice but to tie him up in front of the saloon once he realized where the place was. If not for the piano and raised voices, he might have just ridden past the bar without a second glance. As soon as he picked out the saloon, he discovered the smell of roasting beef drifting on the slowly stirring desert wind.

Once his reins were wrapped loosely around a rickety post, Eclipse lowered his head into a trough half-full of dirty, stagnant water and lapped it up as though it had been poured from a babbling stream. Clint scratched the stallion behind his ears and stroked his thick mane.

"You won't be sleeping here, boy. Soon as I find out where it is, I'll put you up in a stable. Right now, I don't think I could find my hand in front of my face if it wasn't attached to the rest of me."

Eclipse would be fine, Clint knew. But that didn't make

him feel any better for leaving the stallion tied up outside a bar after he'd carried him through the desert without giving him a scrap of trouble. The meal Clint had had at his camp suddenly felt like a paltry lump in his stomach as soon as he got another smell of what was cooking inside the saloon. By the sound of it, there wasn't many people inside the saloon. In a town this size, he was glad the place was open at all.

The front door opened on old, rusted hinges, letting out a shrill cry as though someone was pulling the teeth from a cat's mouth. Of the half dozen or so people that were inside, only the bartender bothered to see who'd come inside. Once he saw the unfamiliar face, the portly Mexican topped off the mug he'd been filling and walked to the end of the bar closest to the door.

"Buenos noches," the bartender said with an offhanded wave. "Get you something to drink?"

Clint walked up to the bar, which was nothing more than a few large planks of chewed-up timber thrown across a row of empty barrels. Behind the uncertain structure was a pair of kegs, which had probably been refilled more times than the bartender's teeth had been cleaned, and a shelf of unlabeled bottles made out of smoked glass.

"I'll take a beer," Clint said.

The bartender waddled over to the nearest keg and pulled a tin mug off of a pile behind the bar. After giving the mug a few swipes of the rag, he poured in a generous helping of brew that overflowed down the side, over his fingers and onto the warped wooden floor.

Holding out a callused hand, the bartender grunted, "No tabs here, señor."

Clint tossed enough onto the bar to keep the man happy for a while and then took a sip of his beer. As soon as the liquid hit his tongue, Clint thought about trying to grab his money back. The stuff tasted more like something squeezed from a dirty sock rather than anything meant to be swallowed. It washed around in his mouth like something kicked up after a nasty belch, leaving behind a particularly vile aftertaste.

When Clint looked up from his mug, he found the bartender staring back at him with a broad smile on his face.

"You like it?" the Mexican asked. "I make it myself."

Hoping the bartender had used a still rather than his bladder to produce the stuff, Clint tried to force a smile onto his face. He was unsuccessful. "What's everyone else drinking?" he asked.

The bartender looked around the place and shrugged. "Whiskey or water."

"Can't say as I blame them."

Distracted by another customer, the barkeep turned away from Clint for a second so he could grab a plate of food that had been set onto the bar behind him by a small woman who might have been the Mexican's daughter. He handed over the food and thanked the customer once he'd paid before turning back to Clint.

"*Que?*" the barkeep asked. "I didn't hear that last part."

"Never mind. How about some of that food? Could I get a helping for myself?"

The barkeep shook his head. "No, no, no. Maria needs to get home. It's getting late."

Maria was headed to the back of the room when she heard her name and turned around. She immediately locked eyes with Clint and stopped in her tracks.

"Come back in the morning," the bartender said. "She can make breakfast or even lunch, but not now . . ."

"It's all right, Poppa," she said once she'd made her way back to the bar. "There's still some chicken left. Maybe some biscuits, too." Still gazing at Clint with wide, sensuous eyes, the Mexican girl ran her fingers through long, thick black hair, which drifted across her face like a silky veil.

Even in the dreary light being thrown off by the scattered lanterns hanging from the walls, Clint could see the lithe figure of the young woman as it moved beneath thin layers of brightly colored cotton. Her body looked like that of a fragile doll whose skin had been expertly painted on until it was a flawless shade of creamy brown. Her narrow hips were wrapped in a multicolored skirt, swaying back and forth invitingly as she walked.

"I don't mind fixing another helping," she said to her father. "After all, we wouldn't want our guest to go hungry."

The bartender may not have brewed the finest beer in the country, but he was far from stupid. He stepped in between Clint and his daughter as though he was throwing himself in front of a rifle battalion. "Kitchen's closed," he said gruffly.

Thinking more about the delicious scent of the food rather than the beauty of its cook, Clint slapped some more money onto the bar. "I hate to be a pain in the rump, but I am awful hungry. Here's something for the trouble I'm causing."

The bartender reflexively snatched the money off the dirty planks and shooed his daughter back toward the kitchen. "Anything for a guest," he said with forced politeness. "But she's going home as soon as the meal's done."

The moment the bartender's back was turned toward her, Maria looked at Clint, winked and pointed toward the other end of the bar. Clint looked in that direction and saw a smaller door, which must have led to an alley or possibly into the next building. He nodded to the young woman and walked to a table sitting on uneven legs next to the piano.

He waited there for his food, nursing the beer, which was proof enough of just how low a man will sink when he's stranded in the middle of the desert.

SIX

When the plate of steaming hot food was placed in front of Clint, he took one whiff and realized that it would have been worth crossing the desert without Eclipse's help and downing an entire barrel of the house beer just to sink his teeth into that food. The chicken was juicy and practically fell off the bone the moment Clint touched it with his fork. The biscuits were fluffy and soaked through with butter, and were good enough to wipe away the rank aftertaste of the concoction swirling about in his mug.

It was all Clint could do to keep himself from eating it all so fast that he might choke on it. Even if he had, it would have been worth each hacking cough and every strained breath.

"How is it?" the bartender asked as he walked up to Clint's table.

Looking up, Clint saw the pitcher in the Mexican's hands and stopped in mid-chew. He nodded and mumbled, "It's all great."

The barkeep set another mug in front of him and tipped the pitcher over, starting a flow of clean water. "The money you gave me was enough to cover the meal, but no more beer," he said as he topped off the cup. Suddenly, his eyes flicked over to Clint's with a hopeful sparkle. "Unless you can pay for another drink?"

Clint looked at the water, thinking that somehow, some way the meal had just gotten better. After swallowing, he said, "Uhhh . . . this water will be fine, thanks."

The barkeep looked down at him and shook his head. "Then no more beer for you. Sorry, señor."

It was at that very moment that Clint realized that, not only did the Mexican brew the beer himself, but that he was actually proud of it. By the way he poured the water, the bartender must have thought he was giving Clint the worst punishment he could imagine rather than answer his fondest wish.

Clint waited for the Mexican to waddle away before grabbing hold of the cup of water and draining half of it in one swig. Without the vile aftertaste of the beer, the food tasted so good that it was cleared off his plate in less than three or four minutes. No sooner had he inhaled the last of the biscuits than the plate was being lifted up off of the table by a pair of small, finely contoured hands.

Looking up, Clint saw the barkeep's daughter clearing off the table. From this close, her skin looked even smoother. Compared to the dark hue of her cheeks, the girl's lips resembled the deep red of a freshly plucked rose. She leaned in close enough to him for Clint to feel the passing touch of her hair as it brushed against his face.

"You like it, señor?" she asked in a quiet voice that was just strong enough to reach his ears.

For a second, Clint forgot all about the amazing supper he'd polished off as his mind went straight toward dessert. "I like it very much," he said. "I mean . . . yes . . . it was delicious."

Her full, rosy lips parted in a knowing smile that took away all the girlish innocence she projected to her father. Suddenly, she was no longer the other man's daughter, but a beautiful, vibrant woman with her mind set on getting some dessert of her own. "I'm glad you like it."

"Where are my manners?" Clint said while getting to his feet. "Why don't you have a seat . . . Maria, isn't it?"

The girl nodded once and looked over toward the bar. Her father was involved in a conversation with one of the other customers and wasn't even looking toward Clint's table. All the same, she leaned down and put her mouth close enough to Clint's ear for her lips to brush teasingly over his skin. "Meet me outside," she said. "Just give me a few minutes."

Nodding, Clint took in a breath that was just deep enough to pull in some of the fresh, natural scent of the girl's flesh. She smelled sweet and tangy at the same time and, before he realized what had happened, he felt the quick press of her lips against his before she stood up and hurried off to the back room.

The barkeep watched her go and shot a glance toward Clint. Unsure of how he should interpret the grin on Clint's face, he started to say something, but then stopped when he saw Clint raise the mug of beer and tip the rest of it into his mouth. Responding by raising his own glass of the home-made concoction, the barkeep returned the toast and jumped back into his conversation.

"Who's that?" the local man asked.

The barkeep shrugged his shoulders. "Just someone passing through who doesn't mind paying for the best."

"If you mean that swill you brew out back, I'd say he's been feeding you a line of horseshit. I know I'd rather put that in my mouth than that beer of yours."

Clint stepped outside and took a nice, deep breath of crisp desert air. It took a few seconds, but eventually his eyes adjusted to the almost total darkness so he could get a better look at the town around him. He'd been able to make out the shapes of some buildings and the space where the street was when he'd arrived, but little else.

Now, he could see that the street extended for another two blocks before leading out once again to the open trail. There were some sounds coming from a few buildings down and one street over, but there wasn't much more than the occasional bout of laughter. In a town this size, if the place was open at this hour, it had to be either another saloon or a cathouse.

It only took a few more seconds of patient listening before Clint's heard a woman squealing in bawdy delight. That, along with the rowdy calls of a few boisterous men answered Clint's question as to which of those two the sounds were coming from.

Clint turned his attention back to the saloon and looked up at the sign over the window. It read, JEFE'S PLACE.

From where he was standing, Eclipse snuffed at the air and poked his nose against Clint's shoulder. The Darley Arabian shifted on his hooves and lowered his head as a way of requesting a bit of attention.

"Here you go," Clint said while scratching the stallion's ears. "I haven't forgotten about you, boy. Next thing for me to do is find a place for us both to spend the night."

"Excuse me?" came a voice that nearly caused Clint to jump right out of his boots.

He turned around, fighting back the impulse to draw his gun, and looked right into the startled eyes of Jefe's daughter. The surprise wore off in a second and as soon as Clint relaxed his muscles, Maria seemed to follow suit.

"Sorry about that," he said sheepishly. "I was just talking to . . . ah . . . never mind."

Maria smirked and stepped over to Eclipse so she could slide her hands over the stallion's sleek coat. "Don't worry. I talk to my horse sometimes, too. It can be a lot better than having a conversation with someone who'll talk back."

Clint laughed and looked over at the young woman who was slowly working her way closer and closer to his side. "You've got a point there. By the way, my name's Clint."

"Hello, Clint. Are you on your way to California?"

"No."

"That's where most people are headed that come through here. Most of the time, they only find this place by accident. I just wish that leaving it would be as easy."

"Why would you want to leave here?" Clint asked. "It seems so peaceful. So quiet. You could do a lot worse."

"Sure, but I could do a lot better."

She looked as though she was about to say something else when she stopped short and turned to face the other end of the street. The way her body moved and her head flinched reminded Clint of a deer whose ears perked up at the sound of approaching footsteps.

"Did you hear that?" she asked in a whisper.

For a moment, Clint thought that she was referring to something she'd heard from inside the saloon. He tried to hear Jefe's voice or even one of the other locals inside, but all he heard was the normal commotion that had been coming from that place all night long. Then, as he turned to look in the direction she was staring, he could hear it.

"Someone's coming," Maria said just as Clint was thinking the same thing.

There were footsteps coming down the street, closing in on the saloon at a slow, deliberate pace. Although he couldn't make out the faces of the two men headed his way, the figures on horseback looked familiar enough. And just like the last time, they had guns in their hands.

Clint took Maria by the shoulders and pushed her back toward the saloon. "Get inside," he said.

SEVEN

One of the best things about not being the leader of any kind of group was that folks were not as quick to realize when you've gone missing. Welles learned that for himself when he was in the Cavalry and that fact still held up now that he was serving under Max Hardam.

Welles knew that Hardam had been doing him a favor when he'd told him to check the cathouse for any sign of the stranger. Even though the smart money would have been on any newcomer in the town to hit the saloon or hotel before anything else, Hardam figured that it would be better to spread his men out a bit to make sure the man didn't get away.

Whatever the other man's reasons, Welles didn't much give a damn. What he knew for sure was that he'd been chosen to watch the cathouse because he was on such good terms with all the girls who worked there. And while Anderson was out looking through the stables for any sign of the stranger's horse, Welles was doing his duty the best he knew how.

In fact, he did it so well that it only took him about three minutes to look around Miss Tammy's Social Club enough for him to know that nobody was there that didn't have any business there. In fact, he had some business of his own to take care of.

"Evenin', Danny," Miss Tammy said as she came strolling down the stairs.

A slender Chinese woman with soft, pearly skin and a long mane of straight black hair, the house's madam was dressed in a form-fitting dress made out of shimmering red silk. Long black gloves covered her hands and went all the way up to her elbows. She moved down the stairs as though she was somehow floating over the wooden slats and the closer she got to Welles, the wider her smile became.

Extending a hand, she said in a vaguely accented voice, "Back so soon?"

Welles took her hand and kissed her first two satin-covered knuckles. "Actually, I'm looking for someone. A stranger. You seen anyone in here you don't recognize?"

Her finely tapered eyes blinked once before flitting around to the girls that were standing nearby. "I haven't seen much of anyone tonight. But maybe one of the other ladies?"

"They haven't, either," Welles interrupted. "I already asked."

"Then there you have it. Was there anything else I can help you with?"

Still holding onto her hand, Welles stepped up close to the Chinese woman until he could feel the smooth touch of her body against his. Her name was Su Tam Mi, but everyone in town called her Tammy. Seeing as how a big part of her business involved not disagreeing with what people said, she never bother correcting them and the name had stuck. Welles liked to call her by her real name every so often just to see the warm look that would come onto her face. When that stopped getting him free turns upstairs, he called her Tammy just like everyone else.

"I need to look for something . . . upstairs," he said.

Tammy bat her eyelashes and did her best to look somewhat stunned by his words. "Oh really? What are you looking for?"

"You." Welles closed his fist around Tammy's wrist and pulled her in closer to him. When he did, she took a quick, sharp breath, letting it out as she slammed up against his chest. He knew from plenty of past experience that she liked it when he treated her rough. Actually, there had been a few times when she'd asked him to do something that even made him stop what he was doing and make sure that he'd heard her right. Considering what he was doing at the time, anything that could make him stop had to have been something special indeed.

This time, as her firm, tight breasts bumped up against him, Welles swore he could feel her heartbeat quicken. She tried to free her hand, but not enough so that she could actually break away from him. That was something she always liked to do. Whenever she would struggle, her screams would always get louder and the fire in her eyes would always flare up.

"You want to look upstairs?" she asked in a hurried whisper. "Then I guess there's nothing I can do to stop you, is there?"

"Nope," he said. "I won't let you or anyone else get in my way."

Instinctively, her eyes darted down toward the growing bulge in his crotch as her free hand reached out to stroke between his legs. Her satin-covered fingers massaged him expertly until his eyes began to glaze over and his grip on her became even tighter. With a flick of her head, she whipped her hair around so that it came away from her face to give Welles a perfect view of her perfectly sculpted features and smooth, high cheekbones.

While taking a step backwards, she looked up at him with wide eyes that all but screamed out from him to pull the clothes away from her body and said, "Then let me take you upstairs . . . you can have anything you want, just please don't hurt me . . . too much."

Each one of her words built up like a series of kisses pressed directly onto the insides of his thighs. By the time he put his foot onto the first stair, she had already broken away from him, turned around and dashed up to the second floor.

EIGHT

Hardam and Bosner rode toward the saloon, watching as the stranger they'd been looking for turned around to face them. As soon as they knew they'd been spotted, each rider drew their gun and brought their horses to a stop.

"Where the hell are Welles and the kid?" Bosner asked in a harsh whisper.

Hardam pulled back the hammer of his pistol and rested the gun on his knee. "I was just wondering the same thing, myself," he replied. "He should be on his way, though."

"He'd better be. Otherwise, I'll track him down and put them both out of their misery." Although his eyes were somewhat used to the pitch blackness, Bosner still had to strain them to get a good look at the pair in front of the saloon. "Who's that with him?"

"Looks like a woman, but I can't be sure. Just stay here where he can't see you too well, and get ready."

Hardam snapped his reins and sent his horse closer to the saloon until he could get a clear look at Clint and Maria. Keeping his gun hidden behind the horse's head, Hardam leaned forward in his saddle and stared directly into the stranger's eyes.

Clint had distinctly seen the faint light of the moon glinting off of metal when he'd first spotted the riders, but now that one of them was closer, he could only make out a gun in the hands of the one who'd stayed behind. Trusting his instincts over his eyes, Clint figured that the man approaching him now simply had his gun hidden away. When the figure got closer, Clint's suspicions were confirmed. These were the same men who'd forced him out of his campsite.

Without taking his eyes away from the men, Clint turned just enough to direct his voice over his shoulder at the girl. "Do you know who these men are?" he asked.

"That one's Max Hardam," she answered while pointing to the closest figure. "The rest of his men are never far away from him, so the other two must be around here somewhere."

Clint had been hoping for something a little more useful than that, but it was too late to ask her any more questions. Especially when it would be easier to simply ask Hardam himself.

Hardam brought his horse to a stop about ten feet away from the front of the saloon. He leaned forward slightly as though he was about to spit on Clint and Maria. Instead, he spoke to them in a cool, steely voice. "I thought I told you to head off in the opposite direction. You deaf or just stupid?"

"I was about to ask you the same thing. Or don't you remember how easy it was for me to get the drop on you outside of town?"

Clint could hear the distant rumble of another horse coming up fast around the other side of the building. It was still a ways off but getting closer with every passing second.

Hardam shifted to look in that direction, but quickly turned his attention back to Clint. "Near as I can figure it, you came into town because that's what you were paid to do. The old man's money don't spend too well if you ain't alive to get it. Since you can't have it both ways, you might as well choose to stay alive rather than make another try to accept your payment."

Maria drew in a sharp breath and set her hand on Clint's shoulder. "You're here to help Mister Greary?" she asked.

Although he didn't take the time to answer her, Clint stored away the name she'd mentioned for use later on. If he was being mistaken for someone else, he might as well know who he was . . . or at least who he was supposed to work for. Right now, however, the guns being pointed in his direction seemed a little more important than whoever this Mister Greary was or why he might want to hire out a gun-fighter.

"All I want is to be left in peace," Clint warned as his hand drifted to the Colt at his side. "If you can't get that through your head, then I can't get myself to feel too badly if I have to put you down. You've got an easy way out of this, Hardam. I suggest you take it."

Once again, Hardam studied the stranger and thought about what he was saying. He and his boys had run off a lot of men trying to come for old man Greary's money, and this stranger didn't seem like one of them. In fact, Hardam was just about to pull back when he heard those galloping foot-steps drawing even closer. The familiar shape of a man on horseback could now be seen through the murky gloom.

Behind him, Hardam could hear Bosner shifting to get a better look at who was coming and raised a hand to tell the other man to stay right where he was. "I'm a reasonable man," Hardam said to Clint. "So you can have your peace. But just make sure to stay out of my way, because that peace can end real quick if you so much as take a step in the wrong direction."

Clint's hand hung over his Colt like the angel of death. "Mister, I don't even know what direction you're talking about."

"Good," Hardam said while turning his horse around so he could head back over to Bosner. "Try and keep it that way."

The other horse was still coming in fast and by the time Anderson's eager face could be seen in the light that was leaking out of the saloon's window, Hardam was well into the cover of shadow.

Making sure Maria was safely behind him, Clint stepped backward until the girl had no choice but to open the door and walk back into the saloon. He then took a step to the side so that there was nothing behind him but a solid wall.

When the horse finally thundered around the corner and bolted past his position, Clint waited for one of the others to make their move, eyes focused on a point between the horsemen so he could see them all.

Something in the back of Anderson's youthful mind had told him that he was about to miss out on a nice bit of action. He'd come up with nothing at the stable and just *knew* that the others had started in on the stranger without him. After riding toward the saloon and spotting Hardam and Bosner facing down another man, he'd put the spurs to his horse and gotten to their sides in less than thirty seconds.

Ignoring the fact that guns might have already been drawn, Anderson sped past the stranger and went straight for his boss. "You found him," he stated as quietly as he could. "I got here as fast as I—"

"Where's Welles?" Hardam asked.

Anderson shrugged, bringing his horse around so he could face the stranger that had been backed up against the saloon. "Hell if I know."

"Probably fucking that Chinese whore," Bosner grunted.

Looking like a kid who was about to bust with anticipation, Anderson leaned in close to Hardam and asked, "What did I miss?"

"You nearly missed the chance you've been waiting for to show us why we keep your ass around in the first place," Hardam answered bluntly. Motioning toward Clint with a nod of his head, he grunted, "Go on, kid. Kill him."

Anderson swung down from his saddle and began to strut toward the saloon with his hands dropping toward the double rig strapped around his waist. Watching with a surprised look on his face, Bosner leaned to the side and whispered to Hardam, "Mind telling me what you're doing?"

"Just what I said . . . seeing what the kid's got. Also taking a look at what this stranger's made of as well."

Memories still fresh from their encounter at the camp site coursed through Bosner's mind. Mainly, he thought of the lightning swiftness of the stranger's draw. "Shouldn't we wait for Welles in case we need more backup?"

Hardam shook his head. "Nah. I sent him to that cathouse for a reason. He'd just want to protect the kid. By the time he gets here, the kid's test will be over." Looking directly at Clint and narrowing his eyes like a hawk studying its prey, Hardam added, "And so will his."

NINE

As Welles made it to the top of the steps, all he could see of Tammy was a fleeting glimpse of pale skin. Even that split-second view was enough to tell him that she was already naked from the waist up except for the satin gloves that still covered most of her arms. She peeked over her shoulder right before turning into the last room at the end of the hall and then disappearing through the door.

He wasn't sure if there was anyone else up there or not, since all he could focus on was that door as he rushed down the hall, peeling his shirt off as he went. By the time he got there and looked inside her room, she was leaning with her shoulders against the post of her huge, elaborately carved bed with her hands raised over her head so she could lightly stroke the engrained wood.

"You shouldn't have run away from me," he said as he stepped inside the room and slammed the door shut behind him.

Tammy wriggled a bit against the bedpost, causing her dress to slip a little farther down her hips. "Why not?" she asked with a pout in her voice. "Does that mean I'm a naughty girl?"

Welles pulled his suspenders off of his shoulders and let them drop to either side. When he started working the fasteners on his pants, Tammy reached out to grab hold of his wrists in a similar way that he'd restrained her downstairs. Her eyes locked onto his as she stepped forward. Her breasts were small and firm, capped with small dark nipples that were rigid with excitement.

She took another step forward, twitching her hips in the exact way needed to get her dress to slide down another inch or so until a slim line of black pubic hair was poking over the top of the material. As much as he wanted to put his hands on her body, she kept him from doing so, shaking her head back and forth like a disapproving teacher.

"Not just yet," she scolded. Tammy's voice was like invisible fingertips brushing gently down the front of Welles's body. "Before we do anything, you must tell me what happens to naughty girls."

For a moment, Welles couldn't get himself to form the words. Then, as she pressed herself against him, his breath came back and he wrenched his hands free from her grasp.

Welles grabbed her by the waist and pulled her in tight. "First, they gotta learn not to run away when they're wanted."

"Mmmm," she purred while pressing her hips against the bulge at his crotch. "You wanted me?"

"Yes." He'd slipped his fingers beneath the folds of her dress bunched up around her waist, sliding it down until it fell into a pile at her feet. "Very much."

When he ran his hands back up between her legs, he traced a line over the slim, moistening lips of her vagina, lingering there and teasing the sensitive nub of flesh just over the opening. Tammy's eyes closed and she leaned her head back, savoring the feel of his fingers on her pussy, then slipping inside it.

Now, her hands began working on his body as well, tearing his clothes away in a quick flurry of motion until he was naked in front of her. Still wearing the long gloves, Tammy rubbed down the front of his stomach until she had his cock in both hands. The feel of satin against his shaft nearly made Welles's knees buckle and just when he thought he might fall backward onto the bed, she stopped what she was doing and took a step back.

"If I've been a bad girl, maybe I should kiss it and make it better."

Not wanting to break the spell she'd put him under by saying another word, Welles simply nodded and leaned back against the bedpost that she'd been standing at only seconds before. With the grace of a gently falling leaf, Tammy dropped to her knees in front of him and reached up to run her hands between his legs and guide his shaft into her mouth.

Welles forced himself to look down at her and was just in time to see her soft red lips part, allowing her slender pink tongue to dart out and steal a taste of him before closing tightly around the head of his cock. She moved her head forward, taking him inside of her while sucking gently at the same time. As she bobbed back and forth, her tongue slid up and down the length of his penis all the way down to its base.

Inside of a minute, Welles was almost about to explode, thanks to Tammy's ability to lick all of the right spots at exactly the right time. He reached down and entwined his fingers within the black silky strands of her hair and guided her up to her feet.

Her hands drifted up along his chest, teasing his skin with the fleeting touch of warm satin. Suddenly, she pressed her palms against his body and shoved him backward until he fell heavily onto the mattress. Welles hadn't even gotten his wits about him before Tammy was crawling on top of him, holding her head low so she could drag her hair over his body.

"I feel like a bad girl again," she cooed.

Before he could answer, Welles felt the intoxicating touch of her gloved fingers once again wrap around his cock. Holding him firmly, she rubbed his tip over the folds of skin between her legs, which sent shudders of pleasure through her entire system.

"You shouldn't tease a man like that," Welles said.

Tammy opened her eyes just enough for him to see the luscious color beneath the lids. "Who's teasing?" And then she spread her legs open wide and fit his penis inside of her, dropping down until their hips pounded together.

Arching her back until her nipples were pointing toward the ceiling, Tammy reached behind herself and grabbed hold of Welles's thighs and began bouncing up and down on top of him. Every muscle in her legs strained with the effort and when she began grinding her hips back and forth as well, a fine layer of sweat glistened over every inch of her exposed skin.

Even though Welles barely had enough strength to move, he forced himself to raise his head just so he could look at her in motion. Tammy's eyes were clenched shut and her lips were parted just enough for him to see her gnashing her teeth together in pure animal lust. He grabbed hold of her hips and slid his hands around so he could feel the perfect tightness of her buttocks as she impaled herself upon him again and again.

Welles knew that if she kept this up much longer, he wouldn't be able to hold out for more than another minute or so. The waves of pleasure coursing through him were so intense that at times they almost hurt. But it wasn't the kind of hurt that was strictly pain. It was the kind brought about by ecstasy so powerful it taxed his nerves to their very limits.

Sweat was starting to trickle down Tammy's naked body and when she felt Welles move beneath her, the reflexive response was to try and press him back down to the bed. But Welles would not be pushed aside so easily. As soon as he managed to sit up and wrap his arms around her waist, he could tell that Tammy's body was even more weak than his own.

With a throaty grunt, he twisted his body around and pulled her off of him. Tossing her to the other side of the mattress, he got to his knees and glared down at her with fire in his eyes. She turned around with her breasts held low against the blankets. Even though she took a defensive position, the expression on her face was pure carnal desire.

She loved it when he took charge of her.

"Time for you to do what I want," he snarled.

Tammy couldn't keep the excitement from her voice when she asked, "What do you want? Tell me."

"Stay right where you are," he said while moving in behind her and placing his hands on her hips. "Now spread your legs for me."

She did as she was told, raising her little backside higher into the air and pressing her chest into the mattress. Turning her head so she could look behind her, she whispered, "Now what?"

Welles looked down at her body, drinking in the sight of it. Her spine ran in a perfect curve and her bottom resembled a ripe peach. Unable to restrain himself any longer, he fit himself into the warm wetness between her legs and thrust all the way in until their bodies were mashed together.

When he lightly smacked the side of her ass, she gripped the blankets and gave him a wide smile. Tammy kept her eyes on him until she started to feel her climax rearing up inside of her. When the orgasm came, her entire body clenched, gripping his cock tightly and forcing a similar reaction from Welles's body.

No sooner had they collapsed onto the bed than Welles was sitting bolt upright again, his eyes tracking instinctively toward the window.

"What is it?" Tammy asked. "What's wrong?"

Welles held up a hand and pressed it against her mouth. After a few seconds, he moved it away and swung his feet over the side of the bed. "Did you hear that?" he asked.

Before she could answer that she hadn't, Tammy could make out the sounds coming through the window.

Gunshots.

Less than a minute later, Welles was dressed and out the door.

TEN

For a second or two, Clint actually thought that the men on horseback were going to do the smart thing and let him be. Then, when the younger one arrived in a flurry of raging temper and flaring machismo, that hope went right into the breeze like dissipating smoke.

He couldn't hear exactly what the leader of the horsemen said to the youngest of the group, but Clint recognized the look in that kid's eyes well enough. It was the look of someone trying to prove themselves. It was the look of someone full of too much piss and vinegar and not enough common sense. It was the look of an animal getting ready to take a bite out of a threat to its territory.

Clint had seen that look plenty of times, all right. That was the look of someone walking toward the point of no return.

His eyes searched reflexively over the faces and positions of all the men in front of him. As far as he could tell, the other two men who were still on horseback were moving away from the kid. Clint couldn't see much of their faces, but they seemed to be turning away from what was about to happen. That just left the kid himself, who was charging toward Clint like a rhino with a score to settle.

Holding out his left hand as if to keep the younger man at a distance, Clint knew better than to waste his breath with any more appeals to some nonexistent rational side. Instead, he gave a simple word of warning.

"Don't."

Whether or not he was affected by the word, Anderson stopped less than ten feet away from Clint and planted his feet in the sandy soil. He squared his shoulders and fixed his target with an intense gaze.

For the next few seconds, all Clint could hear was the wind churning down the street and Maria's feet shuffling on the other side of the saloon's front door. She must have tipped the others inside about what was going on, because all of the chatter and commotion within the saloon had come to a halt.

It seemed as though the only two living creatures on the face of the earth were Clint and Anderson. Both men knew that number was about to go down by one in the space of a few seconds.

Clint's hand remained perched motionless over his gun, waiting for the slightest provocation before drawing the weapon from leather. Anderson, on the other hand, moved his fingers nervously along the edge of the handles of his guns. Just the fact that he was about to pull both of the pistols at the same time told Clint what an amateur the kid truly was.

That second gun was supposed to be there as an alternative to reloading the first. Unless the shooter could use his left hand just as good as his right, he was doing nothing but putting on a show by firing both weapons at once. Every experienced gunman knew that. Just as every true gunfighter could stand and wait for the best moment to draw for hours if need be.

But not Anderson.

Just as Clint had thought, the kid eventually wore down beneath the increasing weight of each passing second that landed upon his shoulders. And when that happened, both of his hands went for his guns in a desperate blur of motion.

Clint's hand, however, made no blur.

One second it was hanging empty over his holster, and the next it was filled with his modified Colt. By the time the kid had cleared leather and managed to get his thumbs on his hammers, Clint had already tilted the Colt up from his hip and squeezed the trigger. His body had instinctively turned sideways into the classic duelist's stance, which presented an even smaller target to anyone trying to fire on him.

The Colt barked once to spit out a single round amid a *pop* of smoke and sparks. The single round had already begun to burrow through Anderson's skull by the time the kid had gotten around to pulling his own triggers. The guns in the kid's fists went off at the same time, sending their bullets wide to either side.

The rest of Anderson jerked back once as though he'd been kicked in the face by a rowdy mule.

As soon as the body started teetering backward, Clint had turned his attention toward the remaining horsemen. His ears were picking up on yet another set of quickly approaching footsteps.

Already, the other two riders were backing away. By the time Anderson's back hit the ground, Hardam and Bosner were nothing more than shadows fading away into the all-encompassing black. Clint held his ground until he could no longer even see a trace of the other men. He strained his ears listening for any steps coming up behind him or the ones that had been charging in from straight ahead.

Whoever it was that had been coming must have turned away to meet up with Hardam because those steps had also faded away into nothing. Clint holstered his weapon and stepped up to the body laying in front of him. The kid's eyes were open wide, looking into whatever awaited those who were too slow to live. Just to be sure, Clint reached down and took Anderson's guns. At least the pistols wouldn't cause any more trouble.

Turning toward the saloon's front door, Clint heard the creaking of loose floorboards right before the door came partially open. Even though he could only see a sliver of a face peeking out from behind the door, Clint knew well enough who was standing on the other side.

"Stay where you are, Maria," he said. After tucking the

kid's guns into his belt, Clint pushed open the door and stepped inside the saloon.

Everyone who'd been drinking or talking in small groups now stood in one big cluster around the bar. All eyes were on Clint as he walked up to the barkeep, slapped Anderson's gun onto the warped wooden surface and let out a slow breath.

"I'll take a b—" Clint started to say before the lingering aftertaste of the saloon's beer drifted over the back of his tongue like something that had been spit up. "Make that a water."

"Sure, sure," the barkeep said as he rushed to fill the order. "Anything you say."

Clint could feel the locals staring at him expectantly, every one of their eyes pressing against his skin like encroaching walls. After a large mug of water was set in front of him, Clint reached out and wrapped his hands around the cool, dented metal. He took a slow sip and let the liquid trickle down his throat, somewhat soothing him after what had just happened.

The main difference between being a gunfighter and a murderer was how that person reacted to killing another human being. Just because Clint was good at handling a pistol and had killed more than his fair share of men, that didn't mean he took away one bit of enjoyment in the deaths he'd caused. And just because every shot he'd fired had been to defend himself or someone else, that didn't make him forget about all those faces staring back at him with cold, unseeing eyes.

Clint could still see the faces of every man he'd been forced to kill. Although he would have made the same decisions all over again if given the chance, those decisions still had a weight of their own that pressed down on Clint's spirit. Sometimes, they weighed more than others.

This was one of those times.

The kid outside looked so young. He should have had his whole life in front of him. Now . . . that life was over. While it didn't sit easy with him, Clint still knew he'd made the right decision. The only decision.

All of these thoughts had drifted through Clint's mind in the time it took for that first sip of water to wash the bad taste out of his mouth. He took another drink and looked up at the waiting face of the bartender.

"Thanks," Clint said.

The barkeep shook his head solemnly. "No, it's me that should thank you. That kid laying outside . . ." Pausing, the bartender looked as though he was about to go outside and kick the body. ". . . that kid killed three men to prove himself to Hardam. Had eyes for my daughter, too. Lord only knows what he would'a done if he had the chance." Straightening up, Jefe stuck out his hand. When Clint shook it, the bartender looked genuinely honored. "You did the right thing, señor. Don't lose no sleep over that one."

Clint pushed Anderson's gun toward the barkeep. "Maybe you should keep this," he said. "In case any of the others come back looking for someone to kick around for their friend's death."

Jefe took the gun between thumb and forefinger, looking at it as though expecting it to bite his hand. "I just hope I won't need it."

"Yeah," Clint said as he took another drink. "So do I."

ELEVEN

Welles was about to collapse by the time he got within sight of Jefe's saloon. With the cathouse being less than a block away, he'd managed to dash all the way to the bar just in time to see the stranger reach down and pick up Anderson's guns. His first reaction was to charge the stranger with gun blazing, but then he caught sight of Hardam and Bosner.

They would surely be making a move that Welles could back in retribution for losing Anderson. But instead of taking on the stranger, they simply moved farther back into the shadows and disappeared.

Still moving on instinct, Welles forced himself to slow down just as the stranger looked in his direction. Welles could still picture how easily that man had gotten the drop on Hardam and knew for damn sure that without the rest of the men behind him, he would be laying on the ground right next to Anderson if he made the wrong decision.

Welles stopped while he was still in the darkness surrounding the saloon and headed in the direction that Hardam and Bosner had chosen. Keeping his eye on the stranger, Welles could tell that, if he'd been spotted at all, it looked like he wasn't going to be shot at so long as he kept to himself.

With the dim light of the saloon behind him, Welles had a hard time picking the two riders out of the darkness right away. Finally, he could see their silhouettes waiting for him at the end of the street. With his rifle still gripped in his hands, Welles charged up to the shorter of the two riders. It was all he could do to keep himself from grabbing hold of Hardam and yanking his ass down to the ground.

"What the hell happened back there?" Welles asked.

It was Bosner who responded. It was also he who slammed the butt of his shotgun painfully into Welles's shoulder, sending him reeling a few steps back. "Just get a grip on yerself, Danny. The kid took his shot and came up short. That's all there is to it."

Welles was still glaring up at Hardam. In the inky blackness, the rider's face was just a vague outline. Even so, Welles thought he could make out the other man's eyes looking down on him, cool and aloof.

"I know you felt responsible for the kid," Hardam said. "But he still had to answer to me. He wanted to try and take the stranger on his own, so I let him. It's not my fault he screwed up."

"No," Welles snarled. "It's your fault he died. We're supposed to back each other up. I watched both of you turn your backs on him and ride off like a couple of damn cowards!"

In the next second, Bosner was off his horse and grabbing hold of the front of Welles's shirt. With strength fueled by his rage, he nearly lifted the older man from his feet. "You got one chance to convince me not to pull your head off right here and now."

"You're scared of that stranger," Welles said. "You saw just like I did how fast he was and it scares the hell outta you thinkin' that you ain't the terror of these parts no more."

The fire in Bosner's eyes flared up like Welles had poured kerosene on it. His grip on the older man's clothes tightened and he pulled him in close enough to take a bite out of his face.

"Now, now," Hardam said calmly. "That ain't no way to talk, Danny. Just because you were too busy screwing that china doll whore of yours, that's no reason to get all cross at Mister Bosner."

The truth of Hardam's statement cut close to the bone,

causing Welles to clench his teeth and start to bring up the rifle in between himself and Bosner. He'd been thinking that very thing since he'd heard the gunshots and now that the words had been said, they burned into him even deeper than Bosner's eyes.

From above them both, Hardam said, "Let him go, Bosner. We got much more important things to worry about besides a load of dead weight that we're better off without."

Reluctantly, Bosner complied, pushing Welles away with a sharp jab from both hands. Welles stumbled back half a step and clenched the rifle in his fists. He looked up to Hardam and straightened up to regain some of his dignity.

"Just tell me what happened."

"We learned a lot just now," Hardam said. "Like the fact that the stranger isn't working for the old man just yet. But being as good as he is, I'm sure the old man will try to get him on his side."

"So that means we're going after him?"

Hardam nodded. "We're going after them both. Especially after what that stranger did to Anderson."

Welles relaxed a bit when he realized that the kid's death was not about to go unanswered. Glancing back toward Bosner, he couldn't help but feel his courage slipping away at the sight of the bigger man. Bosner seemed to blend in perfectly with the surrounding shadows. His dark skin and long black hair made a perfect cloak to disguise him inside the night. His deeply set eyes and trim black mustache resembled markings on an animal's fur to better help him blend in with his surroundings.

Currently, Bosner stared him down until Welles took a full step back and lowered his head submissively. A lethal smile drifted across Bosner's face at the sight. He could smell the fear dripping from Welles's pores. With a grumbling laugh, he climbed back into his saddle and spat down at the other man's feet.

"Good," Hardam said. "Now that that's settled, we can get back to the business at hand."

Shifting his mind back into the pack mentality, he set aside his spat with Bosner. At least . . . for the time being, anyway.

"Are we going after the old man or the stranger first?"

Hardam started to answer, but then stopped himself. His head perked up as though he'd been hit by a revelation. "Neither," he said definitively. "In fact, we're going to let old man Greary get a hold of this stranger and even put him on his payroll."

"What?" both of the other men asked in unison.

"That's right." Leaning forward in his saddle, Hardam gave a quick look back and forth before spelling it out for them. "Greary's been holing up in that cabin of his, covering his tracks and staying away from what he knows we're after. Why's he doing that?"

Looking over to Welles, Bosner answered, "He's scared."

"Right again," Hardam said proudly. "But once he hears about what happened here and what that stranger did to us, Greary will want to get that firepower working for him. With what he's got to offer, the old man shouldn't have much trouble recruiting, and when he's got that stranger by his side, he won't be scared no more.

"Once that happens, he'll get enough confidence to stick his head out of his little hole and take care of his own business. From there, all we have to do is follow them right to the fortune he's got tucked away."

The hungry smile on Bosner's face only widened the more he thought about Hardam's plan. Welles, on the other hand, wasn't so quick to put himself behind the proposition.

"If we let this stranger go," Welles pointed out, "then how do we get past him? Sounds to me like Greary would have every reason in the world to be confident."

"Fortunately, we're not all as stupid as Anderson was," Hardam said. "Once Greary thinks he's got the advantage, it's just a matter of picking the right moment to hit them. Where they're going, there'll be plenty of better places for an ambush.

"Hell, we won't even have to kill them. After the old man leads them into that mine of his, we just set some explosives and bury them in it. I'll even let you pick which tunnel should be their final resting place."

Welles turned around to face the direction of the saloon

where Anderson was still laying spread out in the dirt. The more he thought about what Hardam had said, the more Welles realized why he'd stayed with the man for so long. Despite Bosner's presence, the four men had always turned a neat profit without getting involved in anything so messy as a bank or stagecoach robbery.

When they'd first heard about Greary's mine all those months ago, Hardam had been plotting and scheming to try and get his hands on it. Now, even though one of their partners was dead, that goal seemed closer than ever to becoming a reality. Also, Welles spotted an opening to complete his own bit of business along the way.

Swallowing his anger and pushing it down to the pit of his stomach, Welles nodded and said, "All right. It sounds good to me."

"Of course it does," Hardam said. "Now we've just got to make sure that this stranger goes along with the plan."

TWELVE

Although Clint wasn't exactly happy about killing that kid, he couldn't get himself to feel too broken up about it, either. The rest of the people inside the saloon, on the other hand, seemed positively overjoyed.

He was offered enough free drinks to drown himself in and if the beer had been any better, he might have taken a few of them up on their offers. But no matter how many raised glasses or smiling faces he saw, Clint noticed that every single person in that saloon was keeping well away from him.

Well, just about every person.

Maria took to sitting at the table right next to him, occasionally sneaking her hand out to touch Clint's arm. Her eyes remained locked on him and she kept her head tilted as though she was just about to let out a slow, adoring sigh. That was when the only other person dared to come near him.

It was Jefe. And he didn't seem happy.

"Maria," he said sternly while setting down yet another complimentary drink in front of Clint. "It's time for you to go."

She looked up at her father and instantly knew better than to say one word in her own defense. Instead, she dropped her hand beneath the table and placed it on Clint's knee.

Maria then ran her hand up between Clint's thighs and settled on his crotch.

"Thank you for helping me," she said while giving him a firm squeeze. "If there's anything I can do for you, just let me know."

Even though he couldn't see what his daughter was doing beneath the table, Jefe was bothered enough by what she'd just said. "You can let me know," the barkeep insisted. "We're all in your debt."

Clint gave the bartender a grateful nod and winked playfully at Maria. "I might take you up on that for another meal or two." To Maria, he said, "But that should just about cover it. I appreciate the hospitality, though."

The main reason Clint had stayed inside the saloon for as long as he had was to make sure that the remaining three horsemen weren't about to come back and tear up the place. Since there hadn't been a sign of them for the better part of an hour, Clint figured that they were saving up their vengeance for some other time.

That was fine by Clint. After the day he had had, even the thought of local killers coming after his scalp couldn't distract him from the fatigue that had settled over his entire body. Getting to his feet, Clint looked over to Jefe and said, "It's been a helluva day. Is there a hotel in this town?"

"Oh, sí," the barkeep said quickly. "The Randall House. Clean beds, and it won't set you back too much."

"Appreciate it," Clint said, tipping his hat. "Guess I'll be headed that way." Even though he hadn't seen so much as a trace of law since he'd arrived, Clint said, "If your sheriff wants to see me about what happened, just send him over."

Clint got directions to the hotel from the barkeep, who was suddenly only too happy to show him out of his place. Although he insisted that everything he'd had be on the house, Jefe steered Clint quickly away from his daughter and toward the front door. All of that was just fine to Clint, especially since the entire day seemed to be weighing down on his shoulders like a sack full of rocks.

The hotel was only a couple blocks away, but without so much as a single street light to guide his way, Clint felt as though he'd been walking for miles with a blindfold tied around his face. Every once in a great while, there would be a sputtering lantern hanging from the front of a building, but for the most part Clint needed to keep his eyes strained to pick up what little light the moon had to offer.

By the time his eyes had become somewhat adjusted to the gloom, he was coming up on another lantern hanging like a beacon in the pitch. Just above that lantern was a sign that read RANDALL HOUSE HOTEL. Clint paused for a second before stepping up to the front door.

For the entire duration of his walk, he'd been certain about two things. The first was that he might just be going blind, and the second was that he was being followed. Although the former was only caused from the strain of shifting between the well-lit interior of the saloon to the darkness of night, the latter was brought on by something that worried him much more: footsteps.

He'd heard stories from blind men about how much more potent their other senses became after they'd lost the use of their eyes, which was exactly what Clint was reminded of when he found himself able to pluck the sounds from the air like they were fruit on a tree. What would normally be just another rustling amid the ever-changing background of noise had now become something sharp and distinct knocking against his eardrums.

Clint stood outside the hotel, fishing in his pockets as though casually looking for a match and cigarette. As soon as the steps had drawn close enough, he turned quickly around with his hand flashing toward the gun at his hip. He timed it perfectly so that the Colt was just being lifted from its holster when his eyes made contact with those of his stalker.

Even in the shadows, Clint could see the look of wide-eyed surprise etched across the face of the slender woman who was wrapped in a gray shawl with a scarf tied tightly over her head. There wasn't much else to be seen, but Clint could tell for sure that it wasn't Maria who'd been following him.

"Oh . . . oh my god," came a startled voice.

Unwilling to trust anyone at the moment, Clint kept his hand on the handle of his gun. "What do you want?" he asked.

The longer he stared at the figure, the more his eyes could pick out. Her eyes were still the main things that stood out the most, glinting with reflected moonlight like two gemstones winking at him from a hidden treasure trove. Nearly every part of her was wrapped up tightly in either scarf or shawl, which didn't do much good for Clint's nerves.

"Put your hands where I can see them," he ordered.

She started to tug her arms out of the shawl, but then she sensed the way Clint tensed at the motion. Slowly . . . deliberately . . . she took out her hands and held them up and out as though she was being held up by a train robber. "I . . . I swear," she stammered nervously. "I wasn't going to hurt you. I just . . . wanted to talk. That's all."

Clint stared at her for another moment or two, trying to see if he could recognize her face from earlier in the evening. Although she might have looked familiar in better light, he couldn't place her face at the moment. "Do I know you?" he asked finally.

The woman turned to look over her shoulder before taking a hesitant step in Clint's direction. Seeing that she was plainly frightened by something and was not an immediate threat, Clint took his hand away from his gun and motioned for her to follow him inside the hotel.

Once they were in the brightly lit lobby, she tugged the scarf away from her head and shook free a beautiful mane of cascading curls. Even out of the moonlight, her warm, hazel eyes struck Clint as a truly breathtaking sight.

"My name is Jillian Greary," she said while extending her hand. "If I could have a moment of your time, I'd like to see about making you a rich man."

THIRTEEN

The inside of the hotel somehow seemed much bigger than the narrow front of the building would allow. While the structure wasn't very wide, it was deeper than two places the size of Jefe's saloon. Once they were through the door, Clint could see a long, polished oak desk where the clerk was sitting behind a leather-bound register, a staircase leading to the rooms upstairs and a small dining room area that came complete with a fully stocked bar.

Clint asked Jillian to wait for him at the bar while he arranged to get a room for himself. By the looks of it, there were more keys hanging from a board on the wall behind that desk than there were people in this town. Although Clint hadn't been able to see much of the town, he got the feeling that this hotel was much bigger than it should have been.

He scanned the register after signing his name to it and found three pages worth of signatures from this last month alone. The clerk was a stout man in his late forties wearing the sleeves to his clean white shirt rolled up to his elbows and a pair of wire-rimmed spectacles at the end of his nose.

"Looks like you get a lot of business through here," Clint said.

The clerk nodded once and turned to pluck a key from the wall. "Sure, ever since the railroad started scouting land

nearby, a lot of businessmen have taken an interest in Randall's Crossing."

Clint's first reaction was to ask about where the crossing
was. Thankfully, before he asked the question, he realized
that that was the name of the town. He chuckled a bit to
himself. Funny how little things like that got away from you
sometimes.

When he saw Clint's reaction to his statement, the clerk
looked a bit confused. And since there didn't seem to be an
explanation coming, he shrugged his shoulders and handed
over the man's key. "You're in room number two," he said
while pointing toward the staircase behind him. "First door
at the top of the steps and to your right."

"Tell me something," Clint said. "Is the livery stable close
by?"

"Yes. It's right down the street. At the end of the block."

"My horse is right outside. Do you have someone who
could run my gear upstairs while I take care of my horse?"

Instantly, Clint could see the aggravated look on the hotel
clerk's face. That disappeared, however, as soon as Clint set
a dollar on the desk right on top of the register. "I'm going
out to get my things," Clint said. "I'd appreciate somebody
being out there to meet me."

The clerk looked around and ducked his head inside a
narrow door behind him. "Y-yes sir," he said while searching
his area. "I'll see to it right away."

Clint turned and checked in on Jillian. By the time he
made it outside, the clerk himself was waiting with an expression on his face that made him look only too eager to
please.

"Are those your saddlebags, sir?" he asked, pointing toward Eclipse.

"That's them all right." Clint removed the saddlebags and
handed them over. After a few labored huffs, the clerk reluctantly carried the bags inside. Clint began taking Eclipse
down the street toward the livery and then stopped when he
heard the front door opening and a set of light footsteps
creaking over the boardwalk. Turning much slower than the

first time they'd met, Clint faced Jillian and caught the door before it could slam fully closed.

"The stables are a block down that way, right?" Clint asked, pointing in the direction that the clerk had mentioned.

"That's right. Why?"

"Because that's where I'm headed. I'll be back in a few minutes."

Jillian brought her arms up and wrapped them around herself while looking nervously up and down the street. "You probably shouldn't stay outside for very long," she said anxiously.

"I wouldn't worry," Clint said. "Those fellas took their shot and they'll be licking their wounds at least for the rest of the night. That is . . . unless there's more than four of them?"

"There aren't," she replied immediately.

"Then I wouldn't worry too much for right now."

Still glancing at the street with troubled eyes, Jillian shook her head and held herself a little tighter. "How do you know so much about them? Hardam acted like he didn't know who you were. They never even called you by name."

"I know plenty about their kind. Once you figure out how one of them thinks, you've pretty much got a handle on all of them."

Taking a comforting breath, she nodded her head and let her arms fall down to her sides. "I guess that's why I wanted to talk to you. If it's all the same, I'd like to do that inside."

"Fine by me," Clint said while reaching out to hold the door open. "I won't be long."

FOURTEEN

After making sure that Eclipse was settled in at the livery, Clint stepped inside the hotel and found Jillian waiting for him at a seat in the vicinity of the small restaurant on the other side of the staircase that came complete with a full bar. Besides a bored-looking tender, the bar was practically empty. It wasn't until they'd ordered their drinks that Clint noticed one other couple sitting at a table tucked away against the wall. By the way they were dressed, the pair were employees of the hotel tipping a glass to celebrate the end of their workday.

Certain that anything had to be better than what he'd choked down at Jefe's saloon, Clint ordered a beer. Jillian wanted nothing but a cup of hot tea. When it arrived, she wrapped her hands around the mug and soaked up some of its warmth before taking a tentative sip. The steamy brew seemed to have a good effect on her because when she looked up again, some of the tension had melted off of her features.

The beer was a definite step up from Jefe's mixture, which made Clint feel better as well.

"Guess I should get right to the reason I wanted to talk to you," she said. "I saw how you handled those men, and frankly, we need someone like you."

"We?"

"My father and I. We own a mine outside of town in the Grand Wash Cliffs. Actually, we own several mines, since everyone but my father thought that the area was nothing but a barren stretch of rock."

"And I take it you've found something?"

She looked at him over the edge of her cup and nodded slowly. Steam from the tea drifted in between them like a thin ghostly veil. "Last summer, I came across a vein of gold that should be worth no less than several thousand dollars. At the very least, I should be able to take out some nuggets that could pay for us to move to California and live out the rest of our lives with no worries."

"So where do I come in?"

Once again, a look of worry settled onto her features. Clint almost felt bad for putting it there and spoiling the natural brightness of her smile.

"Hardam used to be nothing more than a conman and two-bit horse thief. Even though my father and I tried to be quiet as mice about what we'd found, somehow Hardam caught wind of it. Ever since then, he's been trying to get my father to tell him exactly where the gold is. He's even taken to threatening both of our lives."

"Surely there's others in town that know about your father's mines," Clint pointed out.

"Sure there are. Everyone in town knows that he bought up all the deeds he could once everyone else lost their faith. Since they've already been down there themselves, most of them don't even believe the rumors about the gold."

"But they know where the mines are. I guess I just don't see why this Hardam person doesn't ask any one of them instead of keeping after you directly."

"Because," she said slowly, "the mines my father bought cover several miles worth of tunnels and caverns. Hardam and the whole town could go through there their entire lives and not find anything. That's why they sold their shares to begin with."

Clint nodded more to himself as he mulled over what he was being told. The questions he'd been asking were more for his own benefit so he could straighten out the situation in his own mind. As the picture became clearer, Clint started to understand the wild happenings that had been going on since he'd gotten close to town.

There was just one more thing he needed to know before all the pieces fell into place. "I'm not the first man you've approached for this job, am I?" he asked.

Her eyes glanced down at the cup in her hands and then went right back up to lock onto Clint's. "No, sir."

"That's why Hardam came after me, then." Clint's mind drifted back to the few times he'd actually spoken to the horseman. What stuck out the most was all the questions about the "old man." "So that's what he's been talking about the whole time."

"All we need to do is get to some of that gold—not even all of it—and we'll be set," she said with the hint of desperation in her voice. "If we could get some protection against Hardam and his men . . . since now there's only three of them anyway . . . then all that's left is a few days of hard work and we'll have all the gold we can carry out of there."

"How many others have you approached with this wonderful proposition of yours?"

For a second, Jillian looked like she'd been caught redhanded. Her eyes drifted away from Clint's as though she didn't have the strength or the will to keep them focused on their target. Finally, she said, "Three."

"And where are they?"

"Dead. All of them."

FIFTEEN

Once again, Clint nodded. He took another sip of his beer and set the glass down onto the table. The couple at the back of the room had gotten up to leave just as someone else entered through the front door. Clint kept his eyes peeled for any sign of brewing trouble, but it was just business as usual for any respectable hotel.

"How did you hear about me?" he asked.

"This may be a small town, but Hardam is well known inside of it. Anyone who shows him up like you did is bound to be picked out of a crowd." She took another sip before continuing. "It's also been my job to keep my ears open for anyone who comes through town that might be a help to me and my father. I'd heard that someone came in alone through the stretch of desert used by Hardam as his own personal hideout, which means that you must've gone through him and his men.

"Actually, I was at the saloon most of the time you were. I just don't think you got a look at me."

"No," Clint said. "I'd have remembered seeing someone like you in that crowd. So what makes you think I'd be any better of a choice than those other three you took on?"

"Because I saw you gun down one of Hardam's own men," she said. Jillian was unable to hide the awe in her voice as she leaned forward and dropped her voice so as not to catch the bartender's attention. "Anderson killed one of the men I'd hired. He was real fast."

A haunted look drifted across Clint's face. The cold sensation in the pit of his stomach was familiar enough and thankfully was just as fleeting. Another swig of beer was enough to temporarily douse the feeling. "That kid was careless," he said while setting the empty glass onto the table. "Careless and stupid."

"Maybe . . . after what you done . . . if Hardam knew you were working for us, he wouldn't even want to bother us at all. He might rather let us go than try to go up against someone like you."

This time, the smile that came onto Clint's face didn't even have the slightest trace of humor. "Come on now. I doubt you even believe that one."

Caught in her wishful thinking, Jillian tried to keep up her air of confidence, but was only able to muster it up for another second or two. When it left her, she slumped back into her chair like a doll without enough stuffing inside to keep her upright. "Maybe not, but even if he does come, you're fast enough to take him. I *saw* you shoot. I know I'm right about that."

Several different things were going through Clint's mind at that moment. First of all, he wondered why he should get involved in something like this at all.

To answer that question, all he had to do was think back to the look in those horsemen's eyes. When he'd first seen those men, Clint knew they'd be willing to kill for whatever it was they'd been fighting for. Now that he knew they were after such a huge stash of gold, he was certain that the lives of this woman and her father were both in grave danger.

"Why not go to the law?" Clint asked. "If your claim's legal, you shouldn't have any trouble getting someone to stand behind you. That's why that whole system was put together in the first place."

"You don't have to tell me that," Jillian said. "If Randall's Crossing had any law, we would've gone to them a long time ago. We've got a sheriff, but he's just the owner of the general store and cares more about cleaning off his shelves than strapping on a gun and doing anything that might get him in any trouble with the likes of Hardam and his men.

"Why do you think Hardam picked this town? He can stay here as long as he wants so long as things remain the way they are. We used to have a deputy that actually tried to do his job, but Hardam ran the poor man down like a dog and all his men surrounding him." Pausing, she got a faraway look in her eyes as though something horrible was playing out in her mind. When she sipped her tea this time, it didn't seem to do any good. "They shot him so many times . . . nobody could save him. Not the sheriff. Not anybody. The whole town remembers that and they're all scared to death of him now. It's like he's the angel of death riding on that horse of his."

Clint gave her a few moments to collect herself before placing his hand on top of hers and rubbing it gently. He hadn't meant to do it, but it just seemed . . . right. Even as his brain told him to give her some space, his body was enjoying the feel of her smooth skin too much to let it get away. With her head bent down over her cup, Jillian's face was surrounded by a thick, wavy curtain of her hair which shimmered with reflected candlelight. It was all Clint could do not to touch that as well before she looked up at him with her wide, hazel eyes and forced a brave expression onto her face.

"I just realized something," she said. "Here I've been talking to you this whole time and I never got your name."

"It's Clint Adams."

"Do you think you could help us, Mister Adams? You'll be paid in a fair share of whatever gold we find. And if something . . . bad . . . happens to me or my father, there's a strongbox with our life savings tucked away that'll be yours after—"

"Keep your savings," Clint interrupted. "I'll help you."

It wasn't the job itself that attracted Clint's attention, and it surely wasn't the gold. What he saw was an opportunity to help someone who was truly in need and who would most definitely fall victim to Max Hardam sooner or later if someone didn't step in on their behalf. Clint hadn't met Jillian's father yet, but he knew plenty about his type as well.

Stubborn, tenacious, bull-headed, idealistic and more than anything else, true to themselves. The sad part was that a combination like that usually got a man killed.

Also, on a deeply personal level, Clint could still feel the sting of being pushed around by Hardam back at his campsite. Even though he could have done whatever he'd wanted at the time, Clint simply didn't like men who hid behind their guns and lackeys just so they could take what hardworking folks had taken time to build up for themselves.

Jillian stared back at him, visibly stunned by what he'd just said. "You'll help us?" she asked slowly.

"Sure. Why do you look so surprised? Isn't that what you wanted to hear?"

"Of course it is, but . . . I've learned the hard way not to look forward to hearing exactly what I want to hear. When you do, that usually means someone wants something out of you." Lowering her head as though she'd just comprehended what she'd said, Jillian took a breath and seemed to darken somewhat. When she looked back up at him, she asked, "What is it you want, Mister Adams?"

Surprisingly enough, Clint hadn't even thought about that part of the deal. He wasn't accustomed to asking for a fee when he gave his help to someone, but life on the open trail didn't come free. After another few moment's contemplation, he said, "How's ten percent of whatever we take out of that mine. Less if my presence alone is enough to put the fear of God into Hardam and his men."

SIXTEEN

For a second, Jillian looked as though she didn't know how to react. Then, when she saw Clint's smirk, she started to laugh at his bravado. "That sounds fair enough to me," she said, sounding relieved. "Actually, I was prepared to offer you more. Truth be told . . . if things go as roughly as I think they might, I wouldn't feel right paying you less than at least a quarter interest."

"Let's just hope for the best. When this whole thing is over, if I did enough to earn more than ten percent, I'll take it."

Jillian held her hand out and looked Clint straight in the eye. When he put his hand into hers, Clint felt a surprisingly firm grip and a single, sharp shake.

"Mind if I ask you a question?" she said.

"Not at all. Especially since I'm working for you now."

Taking in the last bit of tea with one sip, Jillian let the warm liquid trickle down her throat, soothing her spirit as it went. Some of the nervousness from before was creeping back into her demeanor and her voice lowered to an almost timid tone. "A lot of other men I gave this proposition to have asked me for a . . . different price. I've never agreed to terms like those, but in this case . . ." Her voice trailed off and a bit of red flushed into her cheeks. "In this case . . . I might not have minded."

Smiling warmly at her, Clint looked deeply into her hazel eyes, watching how they went from more brown in color to more green depending on just how the light hit them. She didn't appear to mind his attentions one bit. In fact, although the silence between them became deeper and more intense, it never became uncomfortable.

"You're a beautiful woman, Jillian," he said after a while. "And I would never dream of putting you in that kind of position." Taking the last pull from his beer, Clint got up and set some money down on the table to cover the drinks. "But I can guarantee you one thing. I'll be dreaming of plenty of other positions I'd much rather prefer."

Rather than look embarrassed, Jillian tilted her head down just a bit and raised her eyes to look up at him. Whether she meant to or not, her hair fell across her face in a way that made her skin look even softer and her eyes even browner.

"My father will want to meet you," she said, purposefully throwing the conversation off its current track. "How about I bring him here for breakfast tomorrow around seven?"

"I'll be looking forward to it."

Now, she stood up and began walking for the door. Before she got too far away from him, she stopped and looked over her shoulder. "See you tomorrow, Clint. Sweet dreams."

The bartender stood in his place behind the highly polished wooden countertop and kept his back to the couple sitting at the table in a secluded part of the room. He occupied himself by such tasks as cleaning off the glasses that had been dirtied throughout the day, straightening the liquor bottles lined up on a shelf in front of a mirror that took up most of the wall behind the bar, and of course doing his best to listen in on what those two were talking about.

Not that the bartender was a particularly nosy person. In fact, he didn't even know who the hell Miss Greary was sitting with and didn't much care. That is, until he'd managed to pick up that man's name. The words drifted on the air like a couple of feathers that kept just out of reach until the bartender strained himself to grab hold of them.

Seeing as how he was intimately familiar with the acoustics of the room, the barkeep managed to position himself in just the right place at just the right time for him to get the information. When he'd actually heard the name, it was all he could do to keep the glass he'd been polishing from sliding right out of his hand and shattering on the floor.

It didn't sound as though Miss Greary knew who Clint Adams was, but the barkeep sure as hell did. More importantly, Max Hardam would know too.

Hardam had been paying for information from the barkeep for some time, since most of the hired guns that came through town stayed at the Randall House Hotel. Hardam had been especially hot to get the name of this guest and even offered to double the price he normally paid for information that wasn't as hard to get.

Now, the barkeep understood why.

He nodded once to Adams as he went over to pick up the money left for the drinks. Miss Greary was gone by then and Adams seemed to be watching her leave as though he had something on his mind. It wasn't too hard to figure out just what that was since the barkeep had had that very same thing on his mind nearly every time he saw the attractive young woman.

Once Adams had left the bar and climbed up the stairs to the rooms, the barkeep waited until he could no longer hear anybody walking around on the lower floor before ducking into the small kitchen and out a back door. It was getting to be late enough for the time to pull heavily on the corner of the man's eyes with all the weight collected during a long, hard day.

The night was cool enough to slap the barkeep in the face and give him enough energy to keep his head up, but not for very much longer. Luckily, it didn't take long before the sound of approaching footsteps started coming from the far end of the alley. The barkeep turned toward the sound while busying his hands with the task of rolling a cigarette. By the time the paper was sealed, Bosner was standing in front of him with his hands shoved deep inside his jacket pockets.

Putting the cigarette between his lips, the barkeep tried not to look too nervous as the killer approached him and stared daggers straight into his eyes. When Bosner's hand flashed from his pocket, the barkeep twitched reflexively, completely destroying any air of nonchalance he'd been trying to exude.

Bosner's grin had been torn straight from a hungry coyote. He held a match in between the thumb and forefinger of his extended hand, struck it on the side of an empty crate, and lifted the sputtering flame toward the other man's cigarette. "I saw the old man's daughter leave just now," Bosner said. After the cigarette was lit, he kept the match up close to the bartender's face, moving it close enough to his eye for him to feel its heat. With a snap of his wrist, he extinguished the flame and flicked the smoking stick to the ground. "Did you find out what we wanted?"

The barkeep tried not to look too frightened, but he was much better at mixing drinks and eavesdropping than acting. His attempts to save face were almost enough to make the gunfighter laugh.

"Yeah," the barkeep said. "I got the fella's name. B-but first I want the money you promised."

"What's the matter?" Bosner snarled. "You think we're not good for it?"

"No. But Mister Hardam promised me more this time."

"More *if* you can deliver something that's worth the extra fee, that is."

"It's worth it."

Bosner's expression froze over so quickly that it sent sharp pangs of fear into the bartender's gut like little brass-knuckled hands working him over. He was just about to apologize when Bosner pulled his other hand out of his pocket to reveal a fist wrapped around a bundle of cash.

Ignoring the hand being offered by the barkeep, Bosner held up the money and pounded that fist into the other man's chest, knocking him back up against the wall and almost off of his feet. He kept his fist in place, effectively pinning the barkeep right where he was.

"Spill it," Bosner commanded.

"Adams," the barkeep spat out. "The stranger's name is Clint Adams." He waited there uncomfortably for a few seconds, thinking that Bosner wouldn't believe what he'd told him. The bigger man might even beat him, cursing him for a liar.

But instead, the gunman only nodded slowly before easing back and allowing the barkeep to step away from the wall. Turning and starting back down the alley, Bosner stopped and looked over his shoulder.

"Keep this to yerself," he said. "Or you won't be alive long enough to spend this fee."

With that, Bosner threw the crumpled bills in the barkeep's general direction, creating a small fluttering snowstorm of currency.

SEVENTEEN

Over the years, Max Hardam hadn't done very many big jobs in his life. Knowing that it was much safer to take the smaller ones that would come his way, he never found himself on a wanted poster with a price on his head too big for someone to worry about. For the most part, he robbed smaller caravans or the occasional stage. But that wasn't to say that he was a poor man.

On the contrary, he'd stolen enough money to set himself up in a nice spread outside of town where nobody could get to him without Hardam being able to see them from a mile away. It wasn't the biggest ranch in the area, but it was comfortable for someone who'd been raised living in back rooms and shacks his entire life.

He sat on his front porch, too worked up to be tired, fully expecting to watch the sun rise in a few hours. The last half hour had been spent watching a single dot separate itself from the rest of the town and move over the desert, leaving a cloud of dust in its wake.

Even though he'd been expecting company, Hardam reflexively reached for the Spencer rifle that was propped up against the wall next to the front door of his home. The weapon fit perfectly into his hands, fingers resting snugly in grooves that had been worn there after years of faithful ser-

vice. It had been that rifle that Hardam had used to kill his
first man.

And it had been that same rifle that had allowed him to
move out of those goddamn shacks and into a proper home.
The deaths handed out by that rifle were too numerous to
count at this time in Hardam's life, but still the weapon felt
like a warm bit of his own personality given form outside of
his body.

That rifle was Hardam's hot, fiery rage as well as his cold,
uncaring soul.

As the dot in the distance took the vague form of a single
rider, Hardam put the rifle against his shoulder and drew a
bead on the approaching figure. The tip of his finger traced
a gentle line over the trigger and began to apply just enough
pressure to get the taut sliver of metal to move in its well-
oiled groove.

He was slow and deliberate with the trigger, easing it in
the direction he wanted it to go just as he would with a
woman. But before the rifle delivered its promise, Hardam
eased back and let the trigger slip back to its resting place.

The rider was drawing closer now. The sound of hooves
beating against tightly packed sand drifted to Hardam's ears
like a cloud slowly rolling in from the north. Another fifteen
minutes slid by, and he still sat in the same spot with the
Spencer held to his shoulder.

Hardam's arms never got tired. Not when he was holding
the rifle. Especially when there was so much riding in along
with that single approaching rider.

When he could be absolutely sure that it was indeed Bosner that was approaching his house, Hardam lowered the rifle, set it across his lap and waited patiently for the other
man to ride up to the front porch and jump down from the
saddle.

"Must be good news," Hardam said once Bosner was close
enough to hear. "You never ride that fast unless you've got
good news for me."

Bosner strode across the smooth, windblown sand and
climbed the steps up to the front porch. He ignored the rifle
on Hardam's lap, since it would have been more of a surprise

if it hadn't been there. "I guess you could call it good news. It's the news you wanted, anyway, I can tell ya that much."

"Cut the bullshit. Did he get the man's name or not?"

"He got it."

When the rest wasn't said right away, Hardam's anger began bubbling to the surface and his hand closed a little tighter around the Spencer. "You'd best tell me now before I have to reach in and pull it out of you."

Shaking his head, Bosner stifled an uncomfortable laugh. On one hand, he knew that what he had to say meant a whole mess of trouble for all three of the remaining gang members. But then again, he just couldn't wait to see the look on Hardam's face. And the more he demanded the news, the better it was going to be to deliver.

Finally, Bosner looked up and said, "The stranger's name is Clint Adams."

For only part of a second, Hardam's face went blank. Then he shook his head and squinted across at his partner. "You're shittin' me, right?"

"Nope. Even I couldn't have thought of a joke that rich. The barkeep says he heard the man talking himself. He introduced himself as Clint Adams." Bosner let that statement sink in for a moment before adding, "Oh, and that's not all. He was talking to Jillian Greary at the time."

What little shock that had been showing on Hardam's face instantly gave way to cold traces of pure rage. It wasn't the kind of anger that exploded into fits of wild, uncontrolled violence. Rather, it more closely resembled the first stages of a seething, festering kind of hatred that would take a long time to come to a boil and then eventually bubble over.

The feeling was nothing new to Hardam, or anybody who'd ridden with him for any amount of time. When he set his sights on something, he never gave up until he'd gotten it, and this kind of rage was reserved especially for anyone who got in his way.

Old man Greary had been that certain someone ever since Hardam had heard the rumors about the old man's discovery inside his mine. Hearing about this particular instance was enough to make a set of veins stand out on Hardam's forehead. He gnashed his teeth together as if in preparation for when he had them clamped onto Eldon Greary's throat.

"You think he was telling the truth?" Hardam asked in a steely, measured tone.

Bosner kept steady for a second and then nodded. "Normally, I'd say he was full of shit, but after seeing his move twice now . . . it's not so hard to believe."

"I heard Adams was in the area. He was supposed to be somewhere in New Mexico, but that was a few weeks or so ago. As much as I hate to admit it, I think he just might be the Gunsmith."

"So what do we do about it?"

Hardam set aside the Spencer rifle and got to his feet. For the next minute or two, he paced the front porch and threw the occasional glance toward the distant outline of Randall's Crossing. Finally, he wheeled around and asked, "Do you know that he's working for Greary?"

"Not for sure, no. But with what the old man had to offer, I'd say it was a pretty safe bet that he could get just about anyone on his side."

"That's exactly what I was thinking."

Just then, the door to the house swung open and Welles came stumbling outside clutching a half-empty bottle in one hand. By the look in his eyes, it seemed the unsteadiness in his walk was due more to a lack of sleep than whatever amount of alcohol he'd drunk. "Did I hear right?" Welles grumbled. "Did you two say that old man Greary's got the Gunsmith working for him?"

"That's right," Bosner said. "You ever meet up with Clint Adams?"

"Not exactly, but I heard plenty about the man."

Bosner rolled his eyes at the older man and shoved Welles away from him once he got within arm's reach. "Who hasn't heard about the Gunsmith," he sneered. "Now how about you close yer mouth and get the hell—"

"Bosner," Hardam said sharply. "Shut the fuck up."

Bosner's first reaction was to spin around with every bit of the fury he was feeling written across his face. What he found when he looked at Hardam was not just the man who called most of the shots for the small band of riders, but a lean, menacing figure squaring off to him with one hand hanging over the .45 pistol strapped to his side.

Rather than draw his own gun, Bosner pulled himself together and granted Hardam this small victory.

Once he saw the other man back down, Hardam nodded slowly and waved Bosner aside with a sweeping gesture of his left hand. "Go clear the steam out of your skull before you get yourself hurt," he told Bosner. To Welles, he said, "Tell me what you've heard about Adams . . . besides the usual folklore, that is."

Welles took a deep breath and forced his voice to become steadier and more level. Suddenly, the man carried himself and spoke as though he'd gotten a good night's sleep and had never touched a drop of alcohol. "Adams likes to help people. In fact, he likes to help people who're a lot like old man Greary. If I had to place a wager, I'd say that he'll be at Greary's side throughout this whole thing."

At that moment, Welles's eyes took on an intense sheen, like a hawk that had just spotted a slow prairie dog. "I'd even go so far as to bet that he'll go down into that mine right by Greary's side."

As soon as Hardam had comprehended what Welles was saying, he was already thinking of ways to take credit for it. Then again, being the leader of the group, he needed to do no such thing. Instead, he nodded slowly and patted Welles on the shoulder. "You just gave me a good idea," he said with enough force behind his voice that none of the others standing by could so much as consider interrupting him. "Bosner . . . set up a meet with Rattler. We need to call in a few favors."

EIGHTEEN

When Clint woke up the next morning, he might have sworn that he'd somehow wound up in an entirely different town. Without the cover of such inky blackness that seemed to be standard for a night in the middle of the desert, Randall's Crossing seemed damn close to someplace that could be described as quaint.

Along with the sunshine that came through Clint's open window, there was a steady stream of voices engaged in friendly conversations as well as children laughing as they ran down the street on their way to a schoolhouse, which Clint had overlooked the night before.

It was instinct for him to wake up near dawn and this was no exception. Swinging his feet over the side of the bed and setting them onto the floor, Clint stretched his arms and got up to make his way to the washbasin, which was sitting directly in front of the room's only window. He looked out while splashing some water onto his face and was instantly taken aback by the stunning beauty of the desert's sunrise.

The sky was awash in every shade of red and orange he could possibly imagine. Drifting through the window was a breeze that smelled at once spicy and refreshing. There were a few people moving about on the street below, but most of the noise seemed to be coming from the next block over.

As much as he wanted them to stay away just now, memories from the previous night crept into Clint's mind, sending a little wave of paranoia through his system. He reflexively scanned the street for any trace of Hardam or his men. Next, he looked for someone who might be watching the hotel or even trying to get a glimpse of his room. The only thing that made him uncomfortable, however, was the rumbling in his stomach once he caught a whiff of frying bacon and fresh coffee.

Clint knew that Hardam would be after him just the same no matter what he did, so he might as well start the day with a full belly and then worry about the town's problems later. Within a few minutes, he'd splashed some water on his face, threw on some clean clothes and was headed down the stairs.

The closer he got to the small dining area, the more intense the cooking smells became. Judging by the crowd gathered downstairs, the hotel made more of its profits because of their cook rather than the quality of its rooms. There were twice as many occupied tables as there had been keys on the wall behind the front desk, which meant that a good amount of locals were savoring the food Clint had smelled from his room.

While he was looking for a place to sit, Clint felt a weak tap on his shoulder and when he turned around, he saw the clerk that had checked him in staring back with a rather annoyed look on his face.

"Would you care to sit down?" the clerk asked. "There's plenty of folks who want to get in. This *is* our busiest time of day, you know."

"Sorry about that," Clint said as he turned once again to look at the crowded dining room. "But I can't find any open—"

"There's seats for the guests back by the window," the spindly man said with a disgusted sigh. Jabbing his finger toward a section obscured by passing waiters and occupied seats, he added, "Back there . . . by the sign."

Only then did Clint see the top half of a hand-printed sign written on what looked like the back of an old advertisement. All he could make out were the words, HOTEL GUESTS CAN. The bottom half was blocked by a bald man who was big enough to take up at least two regular chairs on his own.

"Guess I didn't see that," Clint said amiably. "Can I take any table back there, or—"

The clerk had already began shoving through the milling crowd to clear a path for Clint. Once he arrived at the sign, he presented it with both arms outstretched and a condescending smile on his face. The bottom half read TAKE ANY SEAT IN THIS SECTION.

Clint picked out a table that was closer to the kitchen and positioned so that he could put his back to the wall and at least two other tables between himself and the picture window facing that street. When he looked up, the clerk had already turned his back on him and was stomping off in a huff.

Even through the noise of the crowd, Clint could hear the clerk's grumbling. ". . . swear, with the type of people we get in here . . . probably can't even read . . ."

The only thing keeping Clint from getting too angry at the clerk was the genuinely mouthwatering smells permeating the entire room. Although the sight of the clerk's strutting back was enough to raise the hackles on the back of Clint's neck, the scent of fried eggs, sausage and biscuits added to the others he'd picked up from before were enough to ease the smile back onto his face. Just then, the kitchen doors came open and a woman who looked to be in her early thirties came rushing through, spotted Clint and immediately started making her way toward him.

Her straw-colored hair was piled up on top of her head and held in place with a fastener made of leather and wood. Although her face was thin and distinctly angular, it brightened up with a wide smile as soon as she got close enough to stand at his side. Leaning down just enough to allow Clint to get a sample of the fresh scent of her skin, she spoke in a melodic voice accentuated with a slight English accent.

"So sorry about that," she said. "Mister Basil isn't what you would call the friendliest of people."

What was left of Clint's anger drained completely away. It didn't hurt that the waitress's peasant blouse was loose enough for him to get a lingering look of her smooth, ample cleavage. "You heard all of that?" Clint asked.

"Didn't have to." Leaning in a bit closer, she winked playfully and lowered her voice to a stage whisper. "If you were with him long enough to walk across the room, that was plenty of time for him to get on your bad side."

It was obvious by now that she was purposely inviting Clint's eyes to roam over her generous curves in an attempt to get him in a better mood. Cheap tactic or not, Clint was in no position to argue. After all, why question something that worked so well?

"Are you the man in room number two?" she asked.

"Actually, yes."

"Mister Adams?"

"That's right."

"Mister Greary and his daughter were looking for you earlier. They said they'd come back around seven which is, well"—looking at a clock hanging from the wall over the bar, she said with a shrug—"now. Should I send them right over the next time I see them or should I wait until you've had a chance to eat?"

"Looks like they beat you to it," Clint said while pointing toward the lobby.

Standing near the entrance to the bar was a solidly built man with a shaggy gray beard the same color as the wispy hair that sprouted from his head like an unruly rat's nest. He looked over the crowded room with sharp, piercing eyes. On his arm, wearing a simple brown dress and a white kerchief tied in her hair, was Jillian Greary.

As Clint waved them over, the waitress lingered nearby for another second and put her hand on his shoulder. "I'll bring you all something to drink. When you know what you want for breakfast, just give a shout. My name's Polly."

Clint watched the old man turn toward him and begin making his way through the maze of servers, tables and chairs. He hadn't made it more than halfway across the room when the clerk came rushing toward him, waving his hands in a frenzy and hissing something that Clint couldn't quite make out.

The old man didn't even break stride when he turned to

look at the clerk and snarl a few choice words. Although Clint couldn't hear them, they were strong enough to stop the clerk in his tracks and drain all the color from his face. It wasn't until the couple were nearly at Clint's table before the clerk found someone else to annoy and charged right to it.

"Honestly, Father," Jillian scolded as they sat down across from Clint. "You didn't have to say that to him right to his face."

"The man had it coming and a lot worse if you ask me," the old-timer replied. "He's lucky I didn't put my boot up his ass just for being such a smart-mouthed pest."

Jillian looked at Clint and gave him a smile that rivaled the brightness of the light streaming in through the windows. When she nodded her head toward the older man making himself comfortable in the seat next to her, she shrugged in silent apology. "Clint Adams, I'd like you to meet my father, Eldon Greary."

"Pleased to meet you, Mister Adams," the old man said while engulfing Clint's hand in a callused, vice-like paw. "Now that all the pleasantness is out of the way, let's get down to business."

"You'll have to excuse him," Jillian said. "Father's not a big one on small talk."

Clint shook Eldon's hand and thought back to the look the old man had put onto the hotel clerk's face. "No reason for excuses. Actually, I kinda like his style."

NINETEEN

Hardam's spread outside of town was even more quiet than usual for this time of day. Although the place wasn't normally a hub of activity, there wasn't even the slightest trace of movement on or around any of the tracts of land. Earlier in the day, Hardam had sold the sparse livestock he'd managed to acquire when the only man he ever did any such business with passed through town. Hardam had needed to get his hands on every bit of cash he could scrape up, and somehow the killer and thief had done so in a legal manner.

What he had planned for that money, however, was far from legal.

As soon as the livestock was led away, Hardam, Bosner and Welles spent the rest of the day riding out to a spot in the mountains that was used as a kind of trading post and hideaway for outlaws on the run. A man with the right credentials could get just about anything he wanted from that little-known spot. Everything from weapons to hostages-turned-slaves were available there.

A man without a familiar face or a friend inside the hideaway got something else entirely: a bullet through the skull.

This haven for the lawless wasn't much more than a collection of shacks that were easily mistaken for an abandoned mining camp. From the outside, the only activity that could be seen was the occasional person wandering to or from one

79

of the dilapidated structures. But that was assuming that there was anyone to see the place at all. In fact, unless someone knew exactly where it was, he wouldn't be able to find the place.

There were hardly any permanent residents here. Only those who were staying for a while to escape from the law or had something to sell were in abundance. Of the handful that remained, there was one man who'd been in this place almost since it had first been staked out by the outlaw community. Not even Hardam knew that man's name. He, along with everyone else there simply called the man Rattler.

Legend had it that Rattler was hiding from one-half of an entire tribe of Sioux who'd cursed him for murdering the other half. According to that same legend, if the Indians ever caught up with him, they'd tie him to a rock, strip the flesh from his carcass and feed him to the snakes.

Rattler was the kind of guy who found the story amusing.

Since the Sioux were only one of several dozen groups out for Rattler's blood, he never left the mountain camp. Instead, he'd decided to stay and run the place. He still had enough friends on the outside to get all the information that was available to him as well as all the supplies he needed to keep the trading post running. These things were better than gold to people who lived and died without the law on their side.

Information was all that separated a good outlaw from a dead one. And there were certain things that just couldn't be bought at any old general store.

It had been a while since Hardam had been up to the old trading post. Even so, as soon as he stepped within sight of the place, he was recognized by one of the sentries that had been placed near every possible approach. Anyone else would have seen nothing more than another shape among a collage of them. But Hardam knew where to look and picked the silhouette of the guard out against a backdrop of shadows beneath an overhang of rock.

Hardam raised his hand and kept his horse moving. Bosner and Welles followed close behind. The first thing they saw was a cluster of shacks that looked more like a pile of used kindling rather than anything that had actually been put together. Another hundred feet or so and their ears were assaulted by a barrage of *clicks* and *snaps* of no fewer than a dozen hammers being cocked into place.

All three of them stopped their horses and climbed down from their saddles. Ignoring the eyes that were gazing in their direction, the trio walked straight for the smallest of the cabins. Whenever they got close enough to see one of the sentries, they looked up and held their hands where they could be seen.

"Well I'll be hog-tied and left for dead," came a voice from inside the cabin. "What the hell are you three doin' here?"

Hardam looked to the only guard in sight . . . and smiled.

By this time, Bosner had stepped up to the shack as though he was about to tear the door from its hinges. Welles seemed content with hanging back and shifting slowly back and forth upon his feet.

"And what the hell," Bosner said in a booming voice, "happened to all yer damn manners?"

The moment Bosner stepped foot upon a rickety platform made out of rotted timber and mildewed planks setting in front of the shack, three gunmen stepped out from where they'd been hiding with weapons held at the ready. Bosner treated the armed men as though they were nothing but scenery and kept walking toward the front of the shack.

Emerging from the dusty shadows within the crooked structure, there came a man who completely filled up the front door with a massive, stooped-over frame covered in a ragged patchwork of skins and thick coats. The figure took a step forward so that he could be seen by those gathered outside. By the looks of him, he'd gathered his clothes over an entire lifetime of robbing the dead. Every one of his jackets and coats were scored with old bullet holes and stained in other men's blood.

The boots on his feet were thick furs held together by strands of coarse twine. He wore a holster that was actually two that had been crudely stitched together to create a triple rig that was a bristling mass of guns and ammunition. The body beneath it all resembled a massive heap of clay that had been flattened out on front and back by some giant's hand. His head was a chaotic tangle of dark brown curls sprouting wildly from scalp, chin and cheeks, entwined with the occasional leaf or chunk of dirt.

By far the most distinguishing feature was the ornamentation hanging around the man's neck. It was a cord of knotted cotton, the ends of which hung down to his chest, tipped with two severed rattlesnake tails that made a dry, clattering sound with every move the lumbering figure took.

"I'll ask you one more time," the man said. "What the hell are you doin' here?"

Bosner stood in front of the man for a second, looking as though he couldn't decide whether he wanted to take a swing at him or go for his gun. He chose neither and embraced the man like a long-lost brother instead. "Rattler, you son of a bitch, how the hell are ya?"

Rattler stood like a badly carved statue until Bosner slapped him on both shoulders and took a step back. He then looked past Bosner and locked eyes with Hardam. "I'm still waitin' for an answer. I thought I told ya to never come up this way again."

"No," Hardam said. "You told me to stay away if I knew what was good for me." Pausing, he narrowed his eyes into angry slits and wrapped his fist around the handle of his gun. "Now if you know what's good for yourself, you'll call your men off and try to do a better job acting as a host. After all, you do still owe me for breaking your sorry ass out of that prison in Tulsa."

Rattler didn't so much as flinch when Hardam went for his gun. Instead, he parted his lips in a smile that had more holes in it than Custer's back and let out a howling laugh that shook his entire body. "I remember that place, Max. Smelliest hole I ever been in. And I wound up there after following up on one of your so-called 'sure things.' But what the hell, it's like I always said: If I knew any better . . ."

"You would'a picked a better line of work," Hardam finished.

"Come on up here," Rattler said as he motioned for his guards to head back to their posts. "And tell Welles to drop the sour face. You boys are with family now."

TWENTY

The two men stared across at each other, each one unsure of whether or not he should be the first one to speak. Rather than having one of them make a decision, it took someone else to break the silence that had fallen between them.

"Oh, for pete's sake," Jillian said in exasperation. "Will you stop looking at Clint as though he was about to take a shot at you?"

Eldon Greary sat at the table, nursing a cup of coffee that had just been set in front of him by their waitress, Polly. He watched Clint shift uneasily in his seat and then shot a glance at his daughter that was full of scorn. "Forgive me, Mister Adams," he said finally. "But I'm not accustomed to dealing with gunmen . . . no matter how many times I'm forced to keep their company."

"It's quite all right," Clint said. "I'm not accustomed to being called a gunman."

Despite all his years of fighting for his life against some of the most bloodthirsty characters in God's creation, Clint couldn't help but feel the pressure behind Eldon's stare. The old man had the bearing of a hard-nosed schoolteacher which dug down all the way to instincts that had been burned into every child's core, making Clint feel as though he was surely in trouble for something he'd done. Even the straight line of

Eldon's mouth made Clint uneasy. He knew it was ridiculous, but still Clint couldn't help it.

Mr. Greary had the look down pat. There was no going against a master.

As if she'd been sent to break the tension, Polly came back over with the breakfast Clint had ordered only moments after the Grearys had arrived. The smell of hot bacon and eggs, fresh biscuits and moist cuts of ham hung over the table, bringing a wide smile to Clint's face.

Rubbing his hands together in anticipation, Clint picked up his knife and fork and looked over at Jillian. "You sure neither one of you wants anything?" he asked.

"Quite sure," Eldon replied. Then, somehow, the stony exterior cracked and his eyebrows raised slightly as he peered down his nose at the plate of hot food in front of Clint. "Unless . . . you could spare a piece of that bacon?"

"Help yours—" was all Clint could say before Eldon all but lunged across the table and snatched away the biggest hunk of bacon right out from under his nose.

When the older man stuffed the food into his mouth, he resembled a bear savoring a pawful of honey. Just for a few seconds, Eldon savored the food and was unable to contain his joy. He looked back to Clint, shrugged and licked the tips of his fingers.

"You're a good man, Clint," he said. "Better than any of the others I've had the unfortunate duty to speak to."

For a minute, Clint didn't know quite how to respond. He felt as though he'd seen the other man transform from one thing into something completely different. The taskmaster was gone. The schoolteacher was gone. Suddenly, Eldon Greary was just a man. A man who obviously loved his bacon.

"Forgive my little test," Eldon said. "Usually, when I talk to men about the job I'm offering to you, they feel the need to impress me with their toughness or even try to scare me right off the bat. Do you believe in first impressions?"

Clint shook his head and chuckled slightly. "I did until just now."

"Well I certainly do. You were going to treat me with

respect and hear me out. You didn't try to question the way I carried myself and you didn't look to my daughter to explain my actions. Would you believe that I once had a man start swearing at me when I approached him like this?"

"Actually," Jillian added, "that man told my father to pull the stick out of his ass and say his piece."

Clint felt a laugh coming that threatened to make him choke on the biscuit he'd been chewing. He covered his mouth and took another sip of coffee.

Leaning forward, Eldon looked genuinely offended by the words that had come out of his daughter's mouth. "That's just plain crude, don't you think? I mean, that shows a lack of character that I won't tolerate in anyone I'm to spend any amount of time with. I'd never trust my life to such a man." With his hands clasped on top of the table, he said earnestly, "You're different than that, Mister Adams. You might even be the man I'm looking for."

Nodding, Clint swallowed the food in his mouth and looked between father and daughter. Both of the Grearys stared intently back at him, their eyes brimming with hope. "I'm flattered, Mister Greary—"

"Please, call me Eldon."

"All right," Clint said evenly. "I'm flattered, Eldon, but I still don't know exactly what it is that you want to hire me to do."

Just then, Eldon shook his head and smirked more like one of the children that a schoolteacher would be in charge of instead of the actual authority figure himself. He shot a glance over to his daughter as though he couldn't quite believe what he'd just heard. "Didn't Jillian tell you?"

"She told me a lot of things. I'd like to hear it from you."

"I'll be leading us into one of my mines so I can retrieve a large amount of gold. I'll be doing most of the actual digging while my daughter takes care of the blasting and separating of ore while you make sure that the whole thing goes off without one or both of us getting our heads blown from our shoulders by the likes of Mister Hardam and his men.

"There's going to be at least three hired guns coming after us, since Hardam will most definitely put the word out that we're going to be standing on top of a potential treasure trove. Once those men start gunning for us, you'll be the one standing between them and us."

Clint watched the other man speak, noting every subtle detail in Eldon's face and posture, which might give him away if he was lying or even twisting the truth a bit. It was the same kind of sight Clint used to check for bluffs at the poker table, which came in handy just as many times when there was more at stake than a simple pile of chips.

Eldon lost all traces of humor that he'd shown only seconds before. While he wasn't quite back to the hard, stony facade that he'd put on earlier, he wasn't exaggerating a single word he was saying, either. As far as Clint could tell, the old man wasn't bluffing.

"Make no mistake," Eldon continued. "Hardam will come after us with all he's got. The only question is how he'll decide to do it. He's handy enough with a gun, but I also know he's got three other men working for him. You took care of one the other night, which leaves himself and two more. Considering the cramped quarters we'll be working in, that's more than enough to make sure none of us get down out of those cliffs alive."

TWENTY-ONE

Clint took another couple bites of his breakfast and washed it down with some of the best coffee he'd tasted in a good, long while. "Sounds to me like you've already given the upper hand to Hardam."

"Smart money surely wouldn't be bet on me."

"Then why go after the gold now? I mean, why not just let it sit there until some other time when you can go after it without having to buck such heavy odds? After all, Hardam doesn't know where the gold is, right?"

Eldon took a deep breath and glanced over to his daughter. He appeared to be struggling against some inner barrier that was preventing him from saying any more. Finally, he steeled himself, turned away from Jillian and looked Clint straight in the eyes. "Hardam may not know exactly where to dig, but he's got a damn good idea."

Turning her head fast enough to make it look as though she was reeling from an invisible blow, Jillian looked at her father in disbelief. "What? H-how does Hardam know anything about where to dig? You told me—"

"I told you what you needed to hear," Eldon said plainly. "If you knew just how close Hardam was, you might have gone off and done something stupid before we were ready. I can't have you going off without—"

"When did Hardam find this out?" she asked. "Because he

never let on that he knew much of anything the last time I spoke to him."

With his eyes still trained on Clint, Eldon lowered his gaze to the table rather than look into the face of his daughter. "It—it was a week ago, right after you last had words with Hardam. He and the rest of his men cornered me outside of Jamison's store. They . . . put gun to my head and—" He choked on the words and needed to collect himself before he could get any more to pass his lips. ". . . and he asked me which mines were the ones with the gold.

"I swore he was gonna kill me. He made me bite down on the barrel of his gun . . ." Once again, his voice trailed off as the memories washed over him to remind him of the stark terror he'd felt at that moment. Enough terror to go against what he'd been fighting to hold on to. "I wasn't gonna say anything else, but then he promised that he would come for you the next chance he could get if I didn't give him something. Before I knew it, I told him the name of the mine. I . . . I betrayed you, Jillian . . . and I was too ashamed to tell you what I done."

"Sounds to me like you didn't have much choice," Clint said. "There's no shame in doing something to protect your own life as well as someone you love. The only person to blame is Hardam. Besides, he obviously still doesn't know where the gold is or he would have it by now. And if that's the case, then you managed to bluff him out of his own game even when he was holding all the cards. You must not be a poker player, or else you'd be damn proud of that one."

Although some of the despair had left Eldon's face, he still found it difficult to look up into his daughter's eyes. When he was finally able, he raised his head to find Jillian smiling back at him. Just seeing that seemed to be enough to put the strength back into his soul and the pride back into his heart.

"Clint's right," she said while reaching out to put her hand on top of her father's. "You might have been killed when that happened, and yet you still managed to keep Hardam away from what he was after. And in case you hadn't noticed, I'm still alive and well, so you called his bluff without so much as a scratch to show for it."

Although it was very faint, the slight twitch in Eldon's eyes was still there. Clint knew right then that the old man had, indeed, been scarred . . . if only on the inside.

"I still don't know how I got away from him that time," Eldon said. "But what I do know is that if he gets another chance, Hardam won't let me get away again." Turning to face Clint, he added, "What I'm saying is that this is my last chance to get my hands on that gold and get out with my daughter and myself intact. What Hardam did over the last few days was only a bit of what he's capable of. If he so much as sees me again, he'll come at me with guns blazing and won't stop until he finds out what he wants to know. Even if it means hurting the only thing I value more than my own life."

Clint didn't have to hear Jillian's name to know that she was the one Eldon was talking about. When he looked over to her, Clint could tell that she knew the same thing. Rather than say any more to him, she simply pat his hand again and tried not to show the fear that had crept into the pit of her stomach.

Resigned to his fate, Eldon only became stronger the more he spoke. "If Hardam sets eyes on me, he'll shoot me down in cold blood just to get what I've got."

"But how could you be of any help to him if you're dead?" Clint asked.

"I may not be of much use, but this is." Before Clint could ask, Eldon reached inside his vest to remove a folded piece of paper. Without any ceremony, he unfolded the paper to reveal a detailed map and slammed it onto the table as though he almost wished something would happen to destroy the document. "This is what got me away from Hardam that day, Mister Adams. This map shows how to get to the gold I found and once I told him about it, Hardam let me go."

Turning back to Jillian, he shook his head and whispered, "Can you forgive your father for being a weak old man?"

Clint reached down to the map and snatched it up off of the table, distracting Jillian before she had a chance to say anything in response to her father's question. In two crisp motions, Clint folded the map in half and stuffed it into his jacket pocket where it rested against his chest.

"First of all," Clint said to Eldon, "you don't have a damn thing to be ashamed of. I said it once and I'll say it again . . . you did what you had to do. You told Hardam what you needed to tell him and in the process, you bought you and your daughter another chance to walk away from this as winners.

"Make no mistake . . . Hardam or any of his men would have killed you, Eldon. I've looked into their eyes and I know they wouldn't have any problem killing someone who wasn't able to defend himself. In fact, their kind usually prefer it that way. They nearly killed me for no good reason and the only thing keeping them from doing the same to you was if you could give them a reason not to. You were smart enough to see that and gave them their reason. I believe that's the only thing that kept you from dying that day.

"Hardam knows you're going to make your move and he's doing his best to prevent you from covering yourself in the process. Well now," Clint said as he tapped the spot where the map lay folded beneath his jacket, "you're not the one Hardam's got to deal with. If he wants this, he'll have to deal with me."

TWENTY-TWO

Eldon nodded as a pleased grin drifted across his face. "He might just bring in some heavier guns just to put us away that much quicker. I doubt we've seen every trick up his sleeve."

"After the reception I've already gotten, I wouldn't expect any less."

"Yeah . . . I heard about what happened with the Anderson boy. By all accounts, you made short work of that one." A glimmer shone in Eldon's eye that hinted at the toughness he'd shown upon first walking into the hotel. "But Anderson wasn't the most of your worries."

"I wouldn't think so. Otherwise, you wouldn't need anybody's help."

Seeing the return of the father she was more familiar with, Jillian took her hand off of Eldon's and turned to face Clint. "Bosner is the real killer of the lot. And Welles has been known to pick a man off at more than a hundred yards out. And Hardam's no slouch with a pistol either."

Watching Jillian discuss the outlaws, Clint noticed the way her voice became intense and focused. Even the way she held herself changed when she was talking about Hardam and his men. There was plenty more to her than the soft skin and flowing curly hair. Beneath those things was a iron-clad spirit that didn't take too kindly to watching others walk all over the people she held dear.

With her passion combined with Eldon's strength and cunning, Clint figured this might not be such an impossible job after all. After hearing both Clint and Jillian talk about their thoughts on Hardam and his men, Eldon appeared as though he was thinking along those same lines himself. Most of the shame that he'd heaped upon himself had been replaced by a strong sense of purpose.

"Mister Adams," Eldon said. "I hope you don't mind me askin' you one more question."

"Go ahead. I am on your payroll, after all."

"Why would you take a job like this?"

Clint couldn't respond right away. He looked at Eldon's face and saw something beyond just a simple need to know the short answer. There was something else there that was chewing away at the old man.

"It's a job that needs doing," Clint replied. "That's the best reason I could ever think of."

"It's just that . . ." Pausing, Eldon looked from side to side as though he fully expected the waitress to be hiding behind a cart somewhere listening in on their conversation. ". . . I know who you are. Why would someone like the Gunsmith bother with a man like me?"

Jillian looked over at Clint. She was clearly taken off-guard by what her father was saying. "You're a gunsmith?" she asked. "What does that have to do with anything?"

"Hush, child," Eldon scolded. "Not so loud."

Clint held his hand up and dismissed Eldon's concern. "Don't worry about it. It's not like I'm on the run from anyone."

"I still don't understand," Jillian said.

"Some folks call me the Gunsmith. It's a name I've picked up over the years."

Suddenly, her eyes went wide and most of the color drained away from her skin. Jillian started to say something, but then stopped and started again using a lower, almost reverent voice. "Wait a second. I've heard about you. You're a famous gunfighter, aren't you?"

"Famous might be pushing it, but—"

"I feel so stupid. How could I doubt it after the way you handled yourself with Hardam?" Turning to her father, she added, "This should go so much easier than I thought. With Clint on our side, there's no way that Hardam would dare cross us. We might even be able to spend more times in the mines and dig up more gold."

Although Clint wasn't a superstitious man, he'd seen plenty in his lifetime to make him wary of cashing in your chips before the last cards had been dealt. Whether some folks called it a jinx or just plain old bad luck, if it was going to happen, it would kick in after someone started talking the way Jillian was right now.

Eldon pressed his fingers against his temples and shook his head. Apparently, he was thinking the same thing.

Even though he'd played it down at the hotel, Clint wasn't too happy about Jillian advertising who he was to the entire place. Even under normal circumstances, there were always men out there looking to make a name for themselves by being the one to put the Gunsmith six feet under. For the gunmen in the area that had already been considering doing him harm, for every one scared away by Clint's reputation, there were two more who saw him as the biggest, most profitable challenge of their lives.

But Jillian hadn't meant any harm by what she'd said, so once breakfast was over, Clint excused himself from the table, set up a meeting with the Grearys for later and went upstairs to gather his belongings. When he came back down with saddlebags slung over his shoulder, Clint approached the front desk to pay his bill. Thankfully, the clerk who'd been there before was off bothering someone else for the moment.

He stepped outside into the dry, intense heat of an oven. The skies overhead were deceptively tranquil and pale blue in color, giving not a single hint as to the boiling heat churning beneath them. To make matters worse, the wind was nothing more than a halfhearted sputter of air no more than something created by someone passing him on the street.

Clint couldn't help but look up into the sky as he walked toward the livery, instantly feeling the fiery lick of the sun across his face. Sweat popped out of every one of his pores like an organized charge, making the stifling, dusty confines of the stables feel like a welcome change of pace.

Eclipse stood in the stall closest to the door, eagerly staring at the door as though he'd been waiting for Clint to arrive with baited breath. Taking his time in saddling up the Darley Arabian, Clint enjoyed being in the shade, no matter how badly it smelled, and prepared for the ride out of town. After paying for the stallion's lodgings, Clint led Eclipse out and into the blazing afternoon.

"Sorry about this, boy," Clint said while taking the stallion by the reins. "But we've got a long day's ride ahead of us."

Actually, Eclipse seemed to be handling the sun beating down on his back much better than his owner. The stallion's steps became quicker as he worked the kinks from his legs, which was the exact opposite of Clint's, who'd become progressively more sluggish. In fact, the more he thought about it, the less comfortable he became with heading down into a dark underground tunnel with bloodthirsty killers hot on his trail.

But it was too late to turn back now. Besides, he was the one who'd been wishing for a way to get out of the sun less than a week ago. Suddenly, Clint was reminded of that old warning: Beware what you wish for.

TWENTY-THREE

Max Hardam looked around the rotting walls surrounding him. The small shack he and his men were crowded into tilted in a new direction every time a wind blew down the side of the cliffs. Whenever one of the men inside stepped too far in one direction, the whole place felt as though it would collapse in upon itself.

Rattler sat in a chair that looked as though it had been fished from the bottom of a swamp, reclining like a king upon his throne. Two of his own gunmen stood on either side, waiting for the order to pull their triggers and blow their visitors right through the flimsy walls.

Standing with his back to Welles and Bosner at Rattler's right side, Hardam scanned his surroundings, examining each piece of rotted timber in turn. "This place amazes me," he said.

Rattler smirked while reaching for a smashed cigar he'd been keeping in his vest pocket. "Really?"

"For a place that's filled with so many holes, you still somehow found a way to keep your stink in here thick enough for me to choke on."

"You wanna choke on something?" Rattler grunted while pulling a rusted railroad spike from a pocket sewn into the arm of his coat. "You can choke on this. Hell," he added with a wide, gap-toothed smile, "you wouldn't be the first."

Rattler shoved the spike back into its place and clamped his teeth around his cigar. "So did you come all this way just to shoot the shit, or did you want to insult me some more? You obviously want something, so why not just spill it?"

Hardam ignored the other man's comments and settled onto a small stool, which creaked beneath his weight. Clasping his hands in front of him, he leaned forward and did his best not to look Rattler straight in the eyes. "I thought you said we were family. Can't family just drop by for a visit?"

"You may be family, but you ain't the kind of family a man's glad to see. You're more like my wife's family."

That brought a smile to Hardam's face. "Do I even need to ask?"

"Nah. If I told you what happened to them, it would only upset your delicate sensibilities." He snapped his fingers and leaned to one side, where one of Rattler's men had already struck a match and held it down low enough to light the tip of the gnarled cigar. "Now what can I do for you?"

"I just need a few things for a job I'm taking on. Quite possibly . . . my last job."

Rattler's eyes narrowed like a wolf zeroing in on its prey. After coaxing a few puffs of smoke from the cigar, he plucked it out of his mouth and stabbed it in the air toward Hardam. "You're trying to get something out of me besides supplies."

"And what makes you think that?"

" 'Cause you know I'd outfit you and your men for next to nothin'." When he smiled a little wider, Rattler exposed a few more teeth. The fact that they were crooked and the same color as sour milk was enough to explain why they stayed hidden most of the time. "You got something big planned, and you want my help, right?"

Hardam nodded once and spread his hands. "You got me."

"Then I want to know everything there is." With that last demand, Rattler's face turned into an ugly, threatening mask. His words came out like sharp jabs that snapped Bosner and Welles to immediate attention. "I don't appreciate being put through all this shit and you know it, so how about you start talking?"

"How much do you want to know?" Hardam asked.

"I'll tell you when to stop."

Hardam took in a deep breath and felt the hackles on the back of his neck stand on end. He'd known this was coming just as he'd known there'd be no way around it. This was also precisely why Welles hadn't wanted to come up to this trading post in the first place.

There were plenty of things keeping Hardam from being up front with Rattler. First of all, no matter how much gold there was, he didn't want to split it up more ways than were absolutely necessary. Second, Rattler was just waiting for a haul big enough to pay for him to reenter the world and buy a more comfortable place of his own far away from the prying eyes of the law.

Finally, Hardam simply didn't like the fat son of a bitch. Never had. Never would.

But the plain and simple truth of the matter was that Hardam still needed Rattler's help. He might have been able to get what he needed through other channels if he'd had more time, but time was the one thing he couldn't get through any channels.

"You've heard about the old man buying up all the interests of mines in Grand Wash Cliffs?" Hardam asked.

Rattler nodded. "Sure. I think I might've unloaded a few of my own bad investments on that old codger. Greary was his name, wasn't it?"

"Yes it was. And it turns out that at least one of those mines wasn't such a bad investment."

TWENTY-FOUR

Hardam brought Rattler up to speed on the entire situation as it stood between himself and Greary. He told him about the gold (well . . . most of it, anyway) and he told him about the map in the old man's possession. When he began talking about events over the last few days, Rattler took an even greater interest.

"This stranger killed Anderson?" Rattler asked with a filthy snarl.

Bosner stepped up next to Hardam and smashed his fist against the wall hard enough that the entire shack swayed back and forth as if it was trying to decide whether or not it should just give up its struggle against gravity. Surprisingly, the place remained upright. "He killed him, all right," Bosner said angrily. "Shot him down before the kid even had his gun out."

Rather than be angered by the implication that Anderson had been unarmed, Rattler saw through to the truth beneath the statement. "This stranger . . . he was that fast, huh?"

Bosner had another explosive rant ready to go, but was stopped short by Hardam's arm pushing him back into his original spot.

"Yeah," Hardam said. "He was that fast. And that brings me to why I came to you rather than just find my own supplies. I need some of your men to come with me, and a good stock of explosives."

Rattler leaned back in his seat and looked at the men on either side of him. With every turn of his head, Rattler's smile grew even wider and more grotesque. "You need extra help as well as some firepower to go after some old man, a girl and this stranger? I know he's fast and killed one's yer own but Jesus, Max, you used to be a lot tougher than that."

"One more thing," Hardam said after Rattler and his men had had their fun. "This stranger ain't no stranger. I got a name. He's Clint Adams."

The laughter inside the rickety shack slowly tapered off until there was only the sound of wind twisting through knot-holes to fill the silence. Sounds from the rest of the trading post drifted into the shack as well, which did nothing to distract Rattler from his thoughts.

Finally, the fat man took a deep pull from his cigar and let the smoke drift out through his nostrils. "You're sure about that?"

Hardam nodded. "He said it himself. But I also saw him move. He got the drop on me before I even heard the first sound and that ain't *never* happened before."

Rattler looked over to Bosner, who nodded once in confirmation. He then looked to Welles.

"How about it, Danny?" Rattler asked. "Is this true?"

Hardam could feel the anger boiling up from the pit of his stomach. "If you don't believe me, then just—"

"Shut yer fuckin' mouth!" Rattler roared in a voice that almost knocked over Hardam, his men and the rest of the shack. The fat man had shed his skin to show the cold-blooded killer who had always been underneath. This time when he bared his teeth, they more closely resembled the ones found inside the mouth of an old, wild animal who'd worn them down after years of chewing on the bones of its victims. This was the Rattler that ruled his own little town so well that even the lawmen who knew about it stayed away. And this was the one who'd long ago earned the respect of the outlaw community of the entire southwest.

"I was talkin' to Danny," Rattler said in a somewhat more

controlled voice. Turning to Welles, he said, "How about it, Danny? Was this the same Clint Adams you saw back in Prescott?"

Both Hardam and Bosner turned to look at Welles as though they were setting eyes on his for the very first time. Although a pivotal member of their group, Welles had been considered to be the one who'd seen and done the least. But now, Rattler was turning to him for verification on a man the caliber of Clint Adams himself.

In response, Welles looked back at Rattler with less emotion than he would show to a plate of beans and nodded once. "It was him, all right."

"You weren't even there when Anderson was shot," Bosner pointed out. "How the hell would you know who did it?"

"I was there at the campsite. I saw him good enough."

Hardam was itching to pound his fist into Welles's scarred old face. If not for the attention Rattler was showing to him, Welles would have been tasting his own blood already. As it was, Hardam sucked down his anger and glared at the man skulking in the back of the room.

"What happened in Prescott?" Hardam asked.

Welles simply shrugged one more time. "Not a lot. I happened to be there when Clint Adams passed through. A friend of mine thought he'd try the Gunsmith and called him out. Adams wouldn't fight him right away, so my friend drew down on him in the middle of the street."

Bosner was riveted. "And what happened?"

"Adams shot him in the chest three times before my friend even knew he'd been hit. Probably a lot like what happened to Anderson."

"That's all I need to hear," Rattler said. "If you fellas are fool enough to go charging in after Clint Adams, then I got no choice but to help you poor souls. I still don't see why you'd want more men, though. Wouldn't it make a better story later on if you three went into that mine on yer own and came out with Adams's head?"

"I couldn't give a shit about stories," Hardam replied. "What I want is gold. And the odds of me getting it are even better if I take more men in with me."

"No sense of drama, huh? Fine then, how many men do you need?"

"What can you spare?"

"You can have these two," Rattler said, indicating the men on either side of his chair. "Plus the three waiting outside. But they don't work for free . . . and neither do I. Whatever gold you pull outta that mine, you'd best set aside thirty percent for me."

"What?" Hardam growled. "That's—"

Bosner's hand slammed down upon Hardam's shoulder. "That'll be fine," he said while stepping forward. Giving Hardam a subtle nod, Bosner knew that he'd be hearing about this the minute they left the trading post. But that didn't matter. What did was that they make it down out of the mountains in one piece and without any more holes than their bodies could handle. "We'll be pulling enough out of that mine to go around."

"Now I see why you keep him around," Rattler said to Hardam while pointing his cigar at Bosner. Neither of the other men could figure out which one Rattler was talking to and which he was talking about. "What else?"

Hardam slapped away Bosner's hand from his shoulder and continued with his list. "I'll need dynamite. Lots of it."

"How much you talkin' about?"

"At least a wagon's worth."

Chuckling, Rattler nodded. "When you bring back them boys o' mine . . . bring me back a piece of Adams as well. I can add him to my collection out back."

It wasn't until they were down out of the mountains and on their way to Grand Wash Cliffs before Hardam sidled up next to Bosner and spoke quickly into his ear.

"When we get back," he said. "we're blowing that godforsaken shithole straight to hell. And that fat tub of shit will be the first to go."

"What about them?" Bosner asked, looking over to Rattler's men.

"Adams will cut them down quicker than he did Anderson. And once he's through with them, I'll drop half of those cliffs down on top of him."

TWENTY-FIVE

Clint rode up to the Greary home on the outskirts of town. The afternoon had gotten progressively hotter as every hour passed, but eventually Clint adjusted to the blazing heat. When he brought Eclipse to a stop in front of the well-built little house, Clint found Eldon busily loading his tools and supplies onto the back of a narrow wagon that looked as though it had been pulled from one end of the country to the other. The cart was made low to the ground and was sitting less than ten feet away from a pack mule that looked almost as worn out as what he was pulling.

Eldon looked up from what he was doing, his hand going clumsily for the old Smith & Wesson stuck inside of his belt. When he saw Clint's face, the old man let out the breath he'd been holding and moved his hand away from his gun to wipe a bead of sweat from his brow. "Didn't hear ya coming," he said.

Clint swung down from the saddle. "Then I can see why you needed someone like me to come along."

Eldon looked more than a little put off by Clint's remark. "After digging in the ground for as many years as I have, a man learns to be prepared for anything. Hop on board and we'll be going."

Clint shook his head politely. "I wouldn't want to upset my horse. He'll do just fine."

"That's a fine animal. I'd hate to see him take a wrong step and get hurt."

Scratching Eclipse behind the ear, Clint said, "I think I've taken more bad steps than this one."

Shrugging, Eldon got back to loading the wagon. "Suit yerself. We're leaving as soon as we can. I figure we can get well on our way to the mine before dark."

Clint rolled up his sleeves and grabbed hold of one of the boxes sitting on the dwindling pile next to Eldon. "Guess I'd better start earning my keep, then."

Between the two of them, they got the wagon loaded and the mule hitched up in less than half an hour. By the time Clint had tossed in the last set of lanterns on top of the neatly coiled rope at the back of the wagon, Jillian had emerged from the house with her arms full of neatly tied canvas sacks.

"The food's all ready," she said while walking toward the wagon. "There should be enough in here for all three of us to last a week or so up in those cliffs. You think I should pack any more?"

Eldon scratched his head and took the sacks from her arms. "Nah. Any more than that would be a waste of space. Besides, we won't need more than a few days to dig out the gold." Suddenly, his face lit up as though he was looking at some glimpse of heaven that had just been revealed only to him. "If there's even more than we imagined, we can always come back to re-supply and then make a second trip."

"We'd better make sure we survive the first trip before planning the second," Clint said. Watching the old man get too confident in how easy he thought this job would be gave Clint another gnawing feeling inside his stomach. Maybe he was becoming superstitious, after all.

"Clint's right, Father," Jillian said. "You always told me if you look too far ahead, you'll only wind up tripping on something right under your nose."

Eldon grumbled something to himself and started tying down a tarp over the wagon. It was then that Clint realized that he was being watched.

Looking first over his shoulder, Clint felt that strange prickling at the back of his neck similar to when someone was eyeballing him from across a crowded room. When he was certain there was nobody sneaking around near the house, he turned his attention toward the cottage itself and found the source of the feeling he'd been getting.

Walking slowly toward the cabin, Jillian lowered her head and took another look over her shoulder to lock her hazel eyes directly onto Clint. When she saw that she'd been discovered, she moved the hair away from her face with a smooth wave of her hand. A little breeze caught hold of her light brown curls and made them dance slowly about her head.

Clint realized he'd been staring at her and smiled apologetically. She returned the gesture and then lowered her head so that she was once again hidden by her long, flowing locks. She slowly climbed the steps leading to her front door, giving Clint a lingering view of her firm backside as it twitched back and forth with every step.

". . . shoot at ya?"

The words came at Clint like a fist that had found a blind spot. Only at that moment did he realize that Eldon had been talking to him for what Clint hoped was only a short amount of time. As much as he tried to pull out what Eldon might have been saying, Clint's attention just hadn't been pointed in the right direction to give him any sort of hint.

Rather than try to fake it, he just shook his head and acted as though he'd been engrossed in something else besides ogling the man's daughter. "Sorry, but could you say that one more time?"

Eldon looked up from the bridle that he'd just finished strapping onto the mule. "I asked if you thought Hardam himself would be fool enough to shoot at ya. I mean, he must know who you are. Not that that would've made much difference to the kid he sent your way."

Clint swung up onto Eclipse's back. "With this much money at stake, I wouldn't put anything past him. The fact that he knows my name probably won't do anything but make him all the more fired up to test me."

"It won't scare him off?"

"No. It never does."

Nodding, Eldon climbed onto the small seat at the head of the wagon. "Well, I'll do my best to help you any way I can, Mister Adams."

"That's appreciated. Hopefully you won't regret that decision by the time we get to that mine of yours."

Eldon started to laugh at what he thought was a jibe at his expense. When he saw that Clint was serious, his laughter became more nervous than humorous before fading away completely.

At that moment, the door to the house came open and Jillian strode outside with another bag of food in one hand and half a dozen canteens hanging evenly distributed from both shoulders. "That's the last of it," she said after hefting the supplies onto the wagon. Placing her foot on the front wheel, she hopped up onto the seat and settled in next to Eldon.

"Say goodbye to this ol' house, darlin'," Eldon said to his daughter with a wide, anxious smile on his face. "We might not be coming back at all."

Shaking his head slowly, Clint let the wagon roll on ahead. "I really wish he'd stop saying things like that."

TWENTY-SIX

Eldon turned the wagon toward the edge of town and gave the reins a quick snap. They were on their way and even Clint couldn't help but be affected by the excited anticipation flowing from the old man.

It was almost as though the miner was giving off an infectious piece of himself that saw all the empty pans in the back of the wagon as an opportunity. Each pick and shovel stacked on top of each other was just another chance to hit the mother lode. Once the town was behind them and the terrain became more mountainous than desert, Clint's mind started to race with what awaited them within Grand Wash Cliffs.

Like the Grearys, he didn't think about whether or not they might find anything, but of how much gold could fit inside the wagon and how long it would take them to haul it all away. There were no maybes for the next couple of hours. There were only limitless possibilities.

The small caravan headed northwest toward the cliffs, which loomed ahead of them in the distance. At times, when Clint would focus on their destination, it seemed as though they might never reach the faraway rocks. Like a massive scene painted upon the backdrop of a desert sky, the cliffs stayed always the same distance away, not coming any closer no matter how diligently the animals walked toward them.

But then there were the times when Clint swore he could reach right out and run his fingers along the rockface. Those snuck up on him when he wasn't expecting it, coming in the form of a breath of cool air that smelled as though it had blown in straight from the top of the highest peak to tease him with the intoxicating aroma of hope.

Before too long, the desert gave way to fields of dry pastures and then eventually to long stretches covered by blossoming trees. The horses perked up noticeably and quickened their steps without having to feel the gentle prodding of a heel or strap across their backs. The mule pulling Eldon's wagon bore its load a little easier once the ground beneath its feet softened up. Even Eclipse started to trot toward the green earth and had to be reined in before leaving the wagon completely behind.

As soon as Clint spotted a small stream meandering behind a stand of trees, he looked over to Eldon and said, "Maybe we should take a little break. Give the horses a chance to graze while there's some fresh water nearby."

Eldon glanced up at the sky and noted the position of the sun. "Might not be a bad idea. That way we can push straight on through a few more hours before we start to lose our daylight."

Acting as though he understood every word that had been said, Eclipse quickened his pace toward the closest bank of the stream. Once there, Clint jumped down from the saddle and stretched his legs as the Darley Arabian dipped his nose into the water and started to drink.

Breathing in the fresh, clean air, Clint allowed himself to wander a bit down the stream and simply take in the beauty of his surroundings. It was times like these that reminded him why he just didn't pick a place in the country that seemed better than the rest and settle down. Although it would be a much easier life to lead without having to worry about constantly being on the move and drifting from town to town, there would be just too much to give up in trade.

Clint had never kept track of how many times he'd crossed from one end of the country to the other, or even the number of different places he'd seen. But somewhere in his mind were all the memories he'd gathered from those places. It was amazing how the same sun could set a different way depending on where a man was when he looked up at it. The colors in the sky over the ocean were nothing like those over a prairie. The purple seen above a field of green touched the eyes differently that when it was over a sand dune.

Every one of these memories swirled about inside of Clint's mind, making themselves known in flashes of sight and sound, almost until he thought he too was turning in a slow circle. He lived to collect those moments. That's what the trail was all about. Seeing the sun, stars and moon from every possible angle until a complete picture formed in his head.

He stood at the edge of the quietly gurgling stream and wondered what it would be like to sink roots into one place and stay there for the rest of his days.

He might as well have tried to think about stepping off the side of a mountain and not falling. Either choice seemed equally impossible. In fact, the very thought of giving up the trail and spending his days fixing fence posts brought a grin to his face.

There were footsteps coming up behind him. Clint had heard them approaching for the last couple of seconds and could tell just by the way they sounded who it was that was coming.

"Hello, Jillian," he said without turning around.

For a moment, there was silence. Then, he could feel her hands on the back of his shoulders. She kneaded his muscles, easing away the knots put there after hours of sitting in the saddle.

"I was watching you over here," she said softly.

"I know."

After a little laugh, she asked, "Are your instincts that sharp or is your ego just that big?"

"Actually," Clint said as he turned to face her, "I saw you standing over there looking this way. I guess the rest was ego since I consider myself better looking than my horse."

Jillian took her hands off of him and stepped over to where Eclipse was drinking from the stream. She ran her hands over the stallion's wild mane and then over his sleek coat. "I don't know . . . this is a fine animal."

Even though he hadn't planned on it, Clint found his hands slipping around her waist. Her figure curved perfectly and her flesh felt soft and warm beneath the thin layers of clothing she wore. Her hair rustled against his face and when he breathed in, Clint got a lingering sample of her natural scent.

"I also saw you watching me at your house before we left," he said softly into her ear.

"Does that bother you?"

"Not at all. I like seeing those beautiful eyes looking my way." Glancing up to look toward the wagon, Clint made sure that Eldon wasn't watching them as well. The old man had his back to them and was busy fussing with some pieces of equipment.

Jillian leaned back just enough to press her body against Clint's. She moved her firm backside against him until she could feel his body responding to her. Then, keeping herself positioned in just the right spot, she looked over her shoulder and brushed her lips against Clint's mouth.

"I want to thank you for all you've done."

Before he could respond, Clint felt the soft warmth of Jillian's lips press lightly against his own.

"Thank you," she whispered. Jillian then opened her mouth slightly, just so the tip of her tongue could dart out and tease the inside of his mouth. When her tongue found his, she probed deeply for just an instant before taking a step away from him.

Clint could still feel her skin against his, her body pushed up close to him. When he opened his eyes, he found her staring hungrily back, a wanton smile on her face.

"And that," she said while heading back toward the wagon, "was for what you'll do later."

Clint swung himself back into the saddle and savored the lingering taste of Jillian upon his lips. Suddenly, gold was the furthest thing from his mind.

TWENTY-SEVEN

The only sound that could be heard from the horsemen came from the animals. Their breaths were the only ones breaking the silence hovering over the heads of man and beast alike. Their hooves were the only thing crunching against the earth in a steady rumble that was carried away by the wind only to be lost fifty feet down the road.

There were seven horsemen now, including the men that had joined up with Hardam's group at the trading post in the mountains. At the head of them all, leading on foot with his face turned down toward the ground, was Daniel Welles. Looking at every rut in the soil and the turn of every rock, he was a man completely in his element. He was the finest tracker Hardam had ever known, which was what had kept him in the gang for the last several years.

He'd insisted on silence among the men. Although noise had no bearing on the tracks he found and there was nothing loud enough to distract him from his purpose, Welles simply enjoyed the quiet whenever he could get it. At the moment, with his eyes trained solely on the ground beneath his feet, he could almost block out the others completely. It was an illusion he reveled in since it came around so rarely.

Following behind at a respectable distance, Hardam and Bosner watched Welles go about his work. Riding on Hardam's other side was a man named Jervis. He'd been with

Rattler for so long that he'd almost forgotten what the rest of the world looked like. While most of the other men at the trading post came and went as they would through any other town, Jervis stayed hidden to act as scout whenever someone came to the trading post that didn't belong, or tried to leave before Rattler was through with him.

Jervis had killed more deputies and bounty hunters after he'd gone into hiding than he'd ever done when he was a part of normal society. A slender man with deeply tanned, leathery skin and a large mustache that covered his entire top lip, Jervis looked more like a lawman than most sheriffs. He even carried himself with a quiet dignity that held up just fine even after forsaking his old life to become a recluse in the mountains.

His coal-black hair was parted down the middle and his back couldn't have been straighter unless his spine was tied to a pole. Riding next to Hardam with his eyes glued to Welles's back, he'd spent most of the trip wondering if even he could hide himself from the older man.

"Is he leading us anywhere?" Jervis asked quietly. "Or are we wasting the better part of a day going around in one giant circle?"

Hardam kept his voice down as well, nodding confidently when he spoke. "He's got a track all right. Ol' Danny's better than a pack of bloodhounds."

"Then why's he leading us back toward the mountains?"

Bosner had been watching everything else but Welles, since he had enough faith in their tracker to let him work without studying his every move. As a result, he'd been able to familiarize himself with the area and keep alert for anything else that the breeze might offer. "We're headed in the right direction," he said. "I heard wagon wheels about an hour ago."

Jervis leaned forward to get a better look at Bosner. "A lot can happen in an hour. If they know we're following them, they could've lost us three times already."

"First of all," Hardam said in a stern, level tone, "Welles don't take us on wild-goose chases. He never has and never will. If he'd lost the trail, he would'a told us. And second, who gives a shit if they know we're following them? It don't take a lot of brains to figure we'd have to follow them since we don't have their map.

"But where else are they gonna go? Greary knows he ain't got much time as it is, so why waste it trying to lose us when that would just give us more time to pick him off before they get themselves tucked away where it's safe. He'll head for his mine. It's the only place for him to go."

"And Adams?" Jervis asked. "I suppose he'll just allow us to come right up and take the gold from them."

"I've got plans for Adams," Bosner said. "He's got a hell of a lot to answer for. Anderson's only the start."

Hardam ignored his partner, acting as though he'd already forgotten about who the hell Anderson was. "Adams is a gunfighter. He may know a bit about tracking and he may know something about covering them, but his best bet is to keep an eye on where we are so he can be ready for us once we get there.

"He'll want to keep us close so he can do just that. And as long as he's within a hundred miles of us, Welles will be able to sniff him out."

Jervis saw the self-satisfied smile on Hardam's face and let it stay there for the next minute or so. By the looks of it, Welles seemed to know what he was doing or was very good at putting on appearances. What Hardam had said was nothing that Jervis himself hadn't thought about before anyway, but that wasn't what was foremost on his mind.

"Do you really think you can finish this?" Jervis asked.

Hardam's mind had been chewing on plan after plan ever since he'd seen Clint put the first bullet into Anderson's chest. He thought all the way back to when they'd come across that campsite and used all of that to figure out how fast Adams could truly be.

With all he'd heard about the Gunsmith, Hardam knew to take what he figured and then count on the man being twice as fast. Overcoming such a man was something countless others had tried. For those countless others, it had been the last thing they'd ever tried to do. Because of that, Hardam knew better than to try and out-draw Clint Adams.

He knew better than to even try and sneak up on him or take a shot at him from afar. No single thing would be the end of Clint Adams. Instead, Hardam knew it would take a combination of the right things chipping away at the Gunsmith's armor until a clear shot to the legend's heart was available.

Indeed, Hardam had been thinking long and hard about all of this and now he even had all the tools required to follow through on the plan he'd devised. "Yes," he said finally. "I think I can finish this."

Welles had stopped to examine a part of the trail that split off into three possible directions. The wagon had been leaving behind a distinct enough path to follow, but the terrain itself wasn't the best for keeping a print. Stooping down to check the grass and dirt to see which way the others had gone, he motioned for the rest of the caravan to give him some space.

Hardam reined his horse in and the others followed suit. With Bosner looking on, he grabbed hold of his saddle horn and leaned forward as though scrutinizing Jervis over a card table. "Let's get one thing perfectly clear," he said. "I brought you and the rest of your men along to do a job for me, not to second-guess my decisions.

"If I tell you to go somewhere, you'll go. If I point to someone and say the word, you'll shoot. But you will *not* sit there and try to question what I'm doing. Do you understand?"

Shrugging, Jervis seemed completely unaffected by Hardam's little tirade. Even though some of the other men looked ready to knock Hardam right out of his saddle, Jervis kept his eyes focused and his temper checked. He could sense his own men were itching to put Hardam in his place, but motioned for them to stay put.

"I was just making sure that you knew what you were getting into," Jervis stated.

"I've heard the stories about Clint Adams," Hardam replied. "I've planned everything right down to—"

This time, when Jervis spoke, the words shot out of him like venom. Cold and bitter. "I wasn't talking about Adams.

I meant us," he said hooking a finger over his shoulder to the rest of Rattler's men. "It seems to me as though you've forgotten just who the hell we are."

Hardam came up short for a second. He was still running through scenarios in his mind where he and his men executed every one of his plans perfectly and rode out of the cliffs with gold in hand. When he took a moment to collect himself and think about what was going on at this exact moment, Hardam stared back at Jervis without being able to completely hide the confusion on his face.

Like an animal that smelled blood, Jervis seized the opportunity presented and went in for the throat. "We ain't here to lay down our lives for you and we ain't here to follow every one of your commands down to the letter. If you think you can talk to us like we're working for you, then I'd suggest you take a second to think about what kind of a deal you think you've got with Rattler.

"We're here to help . . . not bow down and kiss your fucking ass. So the next time you address me or any of my men like your slaves, you'd best stop . . . bend down . . . and kiss your own fuckin' ass goodbye."

Hardam looked first at his own men and then at Rattler's. He was suddenly very much aware that he was outnumbered two to one. The remaining three extra men he'd picked up at the trading post glared at him with eyes that bore all the way down to Hardam's soul. All they needed was one word . . . one simple excuse to come after him and they'd start plucking the meat from his bones. He knew Bosner would come to his side, but not before . . .

"It's a simple thing," Jervis said, interrupting Hardam's thought process. "In case you're wondering, there ain't no salvation for you if you make the wrong decision right now. But the good news is that I'm not asking for anything too far out of your means. All I want is for you to look at me and nod your head if you realize what you're dealing with."

There wasn't a whole lot for Hardam to do . . . which was exactly the point that Jervis was trying to get across. For the moment, Hardam went along with the other man and gave him what he wanted. A quick nod. Nothing more than two twitches of his head, one up and one down.

"Very good," Jervis said with a cruel smirk. "Now tell me what you've got in mind to deal with Adams and I'll see if I can help you out. I'm not here to take over. I'm here to help. Just keep in mind that if you follow up on that plan you've been thinking of where you leave me and my men out here with bullets in our hides just so you don't have to pay us our share of the money, we'll kill you while that smug grin is still fresh on yer face and bury you somewhere God himself wouldn't even think to look for you."

TWENTY-EIGHT

Welles had been watching all of this with great interest. He'd seen Hardam give up ground in battles of will like this one, only to come back later and drive a knife into the other man's back that much deeper. But this time was different. This time, Hardam was forced to look at the error he'd made in judgment as if he was a dog getting his nose pushed into his own mess.

Despite the fact that he was still working for Hardam, Welles couldn't help but enjoy seeing his boss get put into his place. Maybe it was because it happened so rarely or maybe it was even because Hardam had had it coming for such a long time. Welles didn't bother trying to figure out which one it was. All he knew was that he was going to enjoy the moment before it slipped away.

"Welles," Hardam barked. "Did you pick up that damn trail or not?"

And there it went.

"I got it," Welles replied.

"Then follow it before they get too far ahead of us."

Welles looked over all the men gathered behind him. The fact that Hardam was possibly seconds away from getting shot off of his horse was plainer to see than the tracks on the ground. Jervis and the rest of Rattler's men were closing

116

in slowly on Hardam and Bosner, waiting for the first reason to pull their guns and go to work.

Turning away from the others while keeping his ears open for any sign of trouble, Welles started walking in the direction the wagon tracks led, pulling his horse behind him. Part of him was dreading every moment, counting down the seconds until the first shot went off.

When nothing happened, he walked a few more feet, anticipating the feel of a bullet burning a hole through his back any second.

He kept walking, feeling the silence wrap around him like a smothering cloak that kept him from taking in one easy breath. But still, the others followed quietly.

Welles felt every second drag by as though time itself was holding its breath. He could feel Hardam's eyes digging a pair of holes through the back of his head, but he could also feel Jervis's threats still hanging in the air over the entire caravan. In the back of his mind, Welles could also see Rattler's filthy, gap-toothed grin as though the recluse was looking down on all of them from his own hidden kingdom.

Hours passed like this until the pressure was almost too much for Welles to bear. Finally, he could sense one of the horses coming up close behind and then keeping pace with him as he slowly trudged along the path.

Welles ground his teeth together, unsure if he should expect to hear Hardam's voice or the single pop of a gun going off in his ear. After a few more seconds, the only thing he could think about was whether or not he was fast enough to draw and turn around before feeling hot lead chew a path through his body.

Taking a deep breath, he moved his hand down to his gun and twisted his head around to look quickly over his shoulder. Behind him, gazing down with hate in his eyes, was Max Hardam.

"Where do you figure they're headed?" Hardam asked.

Although he did his best to hide it, Welles could feel his heart beating as though it was trying to beat its way out of his chest. His hand was clamped around the handle of his gun so tightly that he didn't even bother trying to coax it away. After taking a deep breath, he was able to respond without letting too much of his nervousness show through in his voice.

"If it's a mine they're going to, I'd say it'd be the Grand Wash Cliffs."

The cliffs could be seen in the distance, looming over everything else like an old, watchful parent.

"That's what I thought. Do you think you'd be able to pick up their trail again if we needed to split off and come back later?"

After the exchange he'd heard between Jervis and Hardam, Welles didn't like the sound of that question. Especially since it would put himself right at the head of whatever double-cross Hardam had in mind.

Unable to come up with anything else better to say, Welles nodded. "The wagon they're pulling isn't too hard to find. From what I seen, it looks like they're not even trying to cover their tracks. They're making pretty good time, too."

Welles snuck a peek over his shoulder to see where the other riders were positioned. Bosner was about ten feet behind, while Jervis and the rest were a few feet behind him. He'd seen this happen before enough times to know that Bosner was giving Hardam as much space as he could without being too obvious about it. He didn't have to look, however, to know that Jervis was watching them all like a hawk. By the time he turned back around, he noticed that Hardam was already pulling back on his reins so he could drop back and join the others.

"Be ready," Hardam said so quietly that even Welles almost didn't hear him. "When you get the signal, take us in the wrong direction. Someplace we can lose our dead weight once we don't need them."

All that was said in a rush of words that were grumbled low enough to blend in with the clomping of the horses. Hardam steered back into the group between Jervis and Bosner.

Hardam had a few signals that his men had learned to always be ready for. Now that Welles knew what was coming, he thought of what he was going to do once he saw one of them. He needed to start keeping his eyes open for a spot far away from where they needed to go. It had to be someplace that would give himself, Hardam and Bosner an advantage once Bosner started shooting, since that was almost definitely what Hardam had in mind.

As he led the group along the path left behind by the wagon, a few more options came to mind as far as Hardam's precious signal was concerned. Welles could strike up something for himself that would finally get him away from Hardam for good with a nice piece of change in his pocket. For that, he needed to talk to Jervis without Hardam or Bosner knowing about it.

And then there was the other possibility.

When that one had first entered his mind, Welles started to dismiss it immediately. But then he thought about it some more and it actually started making sense. It was a long shot, but those were the gambles that paid off the most. If it worked, he would not only be free of Hardam, but free from everyone else's debt as well . . . and rich to boot.

But if it failed . . . even if a single part of it failed . . . the best he could hope for was a swift death. Welles wasn't stupid. In his heart, he knew the best he could hope for would just be death. After all, if he stuck a knife in as many backs as he was planning, there was bound to be payback attached unless the plan went off flawlessly.

Rich and free, or dead and buried.

It was one hell of a choice.

By the looks of it, he would at least have the night to make it.

TWENTY-NINE

As the sun began sliding down past the horizon, Clint and the Grearys had traveled all the way to the base of the Grand Wash Cliffs. Although they were still a few miles from the entrance to the mine, Eldon had taken them to a spot that he'd always used for camp whenever he'd gone there before. The woods had grown somewhat denser closer to the rocks, which made for a stark contrast to the desert they'd left behind.

The wagon pulled to a stop at the edge of a clearing that was roughly the size of the family's cabin back in Randall's Crossing. There was already a spot for the fire set up in the middle of the space, complete with a circle of stones piled up around the remains of a wooden frame that could be used to hold meat over the flames. Clint looked around and jumped down from Eclipse's back.

"This is a nice spot you've got, Eldon," he said.

"I stumbled on it the first time I came out this way. It sits right up against the cliffs so nobody can come around on us from that side and there's so many trees surrounding us that the only way to get in here without hacking your way through with a team of lumberjacks is to come in the way we did. At night, it gets so quiet that you can hear every step a man would take. The noise bounces off a them rocks and wakes you right up. Makes for tough sleeping, but at least we won't get ambushed."

Clint walked the perimeter of the clearing, looking where Eldon pointed and searching for ways that Hardam or his men might take to get the jump on them during the night. As far as he could tell, the camp was as fortified as it could be without being a fort. Everything Eldon had said was true enough. The trees would provide enough protection to keep the gunmen from simply riding up on them, and the foliage on the ground would provide plenty of warning if they tried sneaking in. All that, combined with the fact that their backs were to a wall of solid rock made this one hell of a campsite.

God bless the paranoid mind of a miner.

Already, Jillian was spreading branches across the path they'd used to pull in the wagon, covering it with a layer of snapping, crunching alarms. Eldon made sure the wagon itself was parked right up close to the rock wall and then tied up the horses close by.

Clint surveyed the camp a little more, taking the time to think about the men that were surely headed their way. He figured they'd be following in their tracks and rather than try to cover them, Clint knew it would be better to just let them come. Besides, they wouldn't make a move until after they'd reached the mine, which gave them at least that much time before having to worry too much about an attack.

Once they'd started digging, Hardam would have plenty of time to catch up to them and track them down anyway, no matter what Clint did to try and throw them off. Clint knew better than to assume that Hardam wasn't at least as familiar with the cliffs as Eldon was. Besides, even if they did get to the mines and went through their digging without a hitch, it wouldn't be too hard to catch them when they were hauling that wagon back down.

While he normally didn't go looking for a fight, Clint knew that Hardam wouldn't let them pass without one. And if that fight was coming, it was best to let it happen when they thought they had the upper hand. By letting them come right up close and even leading them to where they wanted to be, Clint figured on catching Hardam when he was most pleased with himself. That way, Hardam would be over-confident and make the mistake of coming at him the way he had the last two times Clint had met up with him.

Time was their biggest enemy in all of this. The most important thing to Clint was that Eldon and Jillian get what was theirs and get the hell away from the area without getting themselves killed in the process. With so much money at stake, Clint knew for damn sure that Hardam wouldn't be satisfied with just stealing the gold Eldon had mined. He would want to get all of it and then destroy the evidence. That evidence, of course, was Greary and his daughter.

If Clint could even hold off Hardam long enough for the Grearys to get away without a fight, then that would be all the better. But if there was one thing he'd learned over the years, that was to never expect the best possibility to be the one you got. Until then, he knew he could hold off a man like Hardam. Hell, Clint knew he could hold off ten men like Hardam.

Clint stood at the edge of the clearing, looking out over the path that had just been covered up. He stared out through the trees, imagining that he could look all the way back over the miles that they had covered to the spot where the horsemen were riding. When he thought about Hardam, what struck Clint the most was the way the man had acted when he'd sent Jon Anderson in to do his shooting for him.

In his mind, Clint replayed the scene in front of the saloon where he'd been forced to gun down the kid who'd been so anxious to take on the Gunsmith.

Hardam had sat on his horse and watched. Nothing more. Nothing less. Just watched as one of his men ran headfirst into his own death. Surely, Hardam probably didn't know who Clint was at the time, but he knew how fast Clint was on the draw. And still, he'd sent in that kid to take on Clint. That kid . . . who Hardam himself was probably sure was going to die.

And why would he do such a thing?

By the time Clint had thought of the question, he'd already come to an answer.

Hardam watched.

That was why he'd sent in the kid. To watch and see just how well Clint handled himself under fire. To get a better idea of how big a threat he was. To learn something about the man who, even then, was sure he'd be facing again.

Now that he was certain of Hardam's motives, Clint felt as though he'd also gotten a better idea of the man he was working against. It didn't take much more than physical skill to be fast on the draw or even good with fists or a blade. What separated a fighter from a killer was what was going on inside his head when he acted. It took something special for a man to go beyond just pulling a trigger to actually plotting to snuff out another human life. It took something inside his head that pushed him over the edge into the darkness that allowed him to send another soul into the abyss.

Hardam had shown that he had that certain something that made him even more than a killer. He was not only prepared to kill, but was prepared to sacrifice one of his own men just to get a look at his enemy in action. It was a senseless, despicable act that proved just how low a person could sink.

The more Clint thought about it, the more he wanted to kick himself for being a part of Hardam's plan and killing that kid. But he knew that was senseless as well. He'd had no choice in the matter but to defend his own life. And that, on top of everything else, made Clint even madder.

He'd had no choice.

Once again . . . all a part of Hardam's plan.

Behind him, Eldon and Jillian were busy gathering firewood and setting up camp. Clint stayed right where he was, putting together his picture of Hardam and contemplating what a man like that would do next. Most of the time, second-guessing robbers and murderers was simply a matter of finding out what their next target would be and how to beat them to the punch.

But Hardam, in one simple act of cold-blooded ruthlessness, had tipped his hand to let Clint know that he wasn't dealing with just any criminal. He'd let Clint know that he wouldn't be following the normal rules.

Finally, Clint turned his back on the scene that kept playing itself over and over again inside his mind. In much the same way that Hardam had left his own man to die, Clint now took a breath and let the haunting last expression on that boy's face fade away to join the others that lived in the recesses of Clint's nightmares.

He spent the last remaining hour or two of sunlight fortifying the camp as best he could, setting traps that would set off a ruckus even before any intruder found his way into the trees surrounding the clearing. Once that was done, he could hear the crackle of a fire and smell the beginnings of their dinner being cooked.

There was nothing left to do right now besides eat, wait and sleep. Somehow, Clint had the feeling that it would take a miracle for him to get much of the last item on that particular list.

THIRTY

After a fairly quiet meal, Eldon shuffled off to the wagon, fished out his bedroll from the stacks of his belongings and spread it out alongside the wooden wheels. It seemed as though Clint wasn't the only one with a mind full of troubling thoughts, since the last several hours had passed without more than the barest of conversations between all three people huddled in the clearing.

Even dinner had been a matter of Jillian preparing a pot of stew and warming up some cornbread while Clint and Eldon sat and waited for it with their eyes fixed upon the surrounding trees. Everyone knew well enough just how dangerous this night could be. It might just be the last one they'd ever see, or it might just pass without so much as a peep from Hardam and his men.

Although Clint's money was on the latter, he didn't want to get anyone's confidence up too high. It was a fine line to walk between keeping everyone on their toes and keeping them all too scared to function, but that was why he'd been hired for this job to begin with. Besides, Eldon seemed more wary than anything else, which was precisely where Clint thought he should be. And Jillian kept her eyes on Clint for the most part. After her father had stretched out beside the wagon and slid his hat down over his eyes, she stowed the cooking utensils away and stood next to the fire, staring down at the flames.

Clint had already taken up his position, sitting on a fallen log with his back to the area of trees where he'd laid the most traps that would let him know if someone was approaching. Hopefully, if anyone tried sneaking up on them, they'd be able to see Clint's back and would try to come in from that direction. After that, Clint was relying solely on his speed and aim to see him through.

The Colt hung ready at his side. Clint absently drew the gun and flipped open the chamber to peer inside, rolling the cylinder to make sure every round was in its place.

"You checked that three times already," Jillian said from her spot near the fire.

Clint smiled and rolled the cylinder anyway, knowing she was right, but checking all the same. "It's something to pass the time," he said.

Glancing over toward the leaping flames, Clint couldn't help but be transfixed by the way the shadows played over Jillian's face and body. With the light dancing through her hair, which now hung loosely well past her shoulders, Jillian's skin seemed almost fluid in texture. When she smiled, it was like staring at a statue that had been carved to smooth, elegant perfection and then seeing it come to life. That smile was a miracle. Her voice was a gentle caress to his ears.

Even across the distance that separated them, Clint could see the detail in Jillian's eyes. They looked more green than brown tonight. She turned them away from him and looked toward the trees, shuddering as though she could feel the approaching horsemen.

"How much longer will we have to wait?" she asked.

Clint knew what she was referring to, but didn't want to make her feel any more nervous than she already was. Shrugging casually, he asked, "Wait for what?"

Turning to face him once again, Jillian smiled knowingly and shook her head. She was about to say something else when she looked back toward her father. Eldon lay curled up with his back to the fire. Already, the sounds of his snoring drifted through the clearing.

Jillian walked up next to Clint and spoke in a hushed tone. "You know damn well what I'm talking about. How much longer before they get here? I mean, Hardam and his men will be coming, won't they?"

Clint nodded. "Yeah. They'll be coming."

"Can you protect us against them all?"

With all that Clint had figured out about the horsemen, he knew damn well that Hardam wouldn't just come with the two men he had left. After what Hardam had seen, he would bring something else to surprise them. But since he didn't know exactly what that surprise would be, Clint decided not to upset the young woman looking to him for hope.

"I'm in this just the same as you and your father," he said. "I'll figure some way out. That's why you hired me, isn't it?"

Jillian's face seemed to darken somewhat and she let her eyes drop away from Clint's. "Yes . . . it is."

"So let me worry about Hardam. Besides, I don't think he'll come after us until we're at least inside the mine. Probably not even until we've dug out a good amount of gold."

She perked up a bit after hearing that, but immediately tried to cover up the fact by acting cool and aloof. "What makes you think that?" she asked.

"Because men like him are lazy. It would be a whole lot easier for him to let us do all the actual work while he just sits back and waits until all he has to do is take it from us. If he was willing to work hard for his money, he'd be making an honest living."

Jillian's mouth turned up at the corners in a reluctant smile. Instinctively, her face turned away and she reached up a hand to try and cover it.

Clint reached out and gently took hold of her wrist, pulling her hand away until she slowly looked back up at him. "That's better," he said. "It's a shame to see you try and hide that pretty smile of yours. What's so funny, anyway?"

"Nothing really. Just the thought of Hardam making an honest living. The first thing I saw in my head was him behind a plow, cursing out a stubborn mule."

The thought was just ridiculous enough to bring a smile

to Clint's face as well. More than anything that was actually said, the pair started laughing just because it felt so good to let themselves relax for a change. For the next couple of seconds, they weren't worried about running for their lives. They weren't afraid of death.

There was just the moment.

Jillian did her best to keep her voice down and once she gained control of her laughing, she looked up at Clint. The shadow of her smile still hung over her face like a silken veil. That smile gave way to something stronger: a look in her eyes that was both hungry and nervous at the same time.

When Clint saw that look, it struck at something deep inside of him. It felt like a warm, gentle hand urging him forward until he was leaning down to gently kiss her lips.

At first, she tried to pull away. Then, a soft moan came from the back of her throat as Jillian pressed herself against him and wrapped her arms around Clint's body. She held on tightly as though she was afraid that he might get away from her as her lips hungrily devoured him and her tongue slipped inside his mouth.

Clint's hands roamed over the curves of her figure, just as he'd been wanting to do since the first time he'd seen her. When he slid his hands over her hips, she wriggled back and forth and moaned a little louder. As his hands slipped down to cup her buttocks, Jillian leaned her head back and clenched her eyes shut as though she was about to let out a passionate scream that would echo off the face of the cliffs.

Taking control of herself just before waking her father, she took Clint by the hand and led him off into the nearby trees, far away from the fire, where they could be alone.

THIRTY-ONE

With every step that they took into the trees surrounding their campsite, Clint and Jillian became enveloped in a thick, inky darkness that surrounded them like a blanket that had been cooled by a passing breeze. It wrapped around them and held them tightly, making them feel safe inside its embrace and reluctant to go back into the light.

Jillian held onto Clint's hand as she stepped backward through the shadows, each step following confidently after the other. Not once did she seem in danger of falling or tripping over any of the uneven ground. She moved like a cat walking its home turf, every inch committed to memory.

All the while, she kept her eyes fixed on Clint. He watched as the fading firelight danced over the hazel jewels, and used them as his only guide through the pitch blackness. Her hands closed around his, turning him when he needed to turn until finally her back bumped up against a tree and she pulled him close against her.

"Are you going to protect me, Clint?" she asked in a seductive whisper. "Are you going to make sure that my body is safe?" When she asked those questions, she guided his hands over her hips and then up to her breasts. "Are you going to make me feel safe?"

Still gazing deeply into her eyes, Clint replied, "Yes. I'll watch over you." Now he moved his hands without her help,

129

cupping her breasts and then moving his hands around and down her back. "I won't let anything bad happen to you."

His palms moved over her shapely figure until he got a nice firm hold of her tight buttocks. As he began massaging the finely muscled texture of her body, Clint heard her draw in sharp breaths, letting them out slowly. She leaned in close enough to put her lips on his neck and brush them gently over his skin, flicking her tongue out here and there to add to the sensations she sent down through his entire body.

As Clint took his time and savored the feel of Jillian's flesh, he worked her skirt up until he could slide his hands up underneath it and slip his fingers beneath the soft cotton of her undergarments. As soon as his fingers touched the warm flesh of her upper thigh, Jillian couldn't keep herself from gently biting his shoulder.

It was all she could do to keep from crying out. And the closer Clint's hands got to the warm, moist spot between her legs, the harder she sunk her teeth into him. He felt only the slightest twinge of pain before Jillian placed her hands on Clint's chest and pushed him back.

With only a few feet between them, Clint could see her entire body. Jillian's skirts were rumpled and pulled up at odd angles, giving him a view of one leg all the way up to her hip while the other leg remained relatively covered. The thin cotton blouse she was wearing was off of her shoulders and when she reached up to run her hands over her breasts, Jillian took hold of the material and pulled it down. Her small, pink nipples hardened almost instantly in the cool night air.

"I want you to watch me," Jillian said softly as she reached down to take hold of her skirts. "Watch and tell me when something's gonna happen to me."

It took every measure of self-control that Clint could muster to keep himself from charging forward and running his hands all over Jillian's smooth, exposed skin. The tight curls of her hair fell down over her shoulders to brush up against the pink nubs of her nipples. The way she moved her head slowly from side to side, closing her eyes and smiling ever so slightly showed just how much she liked the feel of her hair against her skin. Her lips parted and she gasped softly as she ran her hands over her nipples and pinched them ever so gently.

One hand ayed on her breast while the other traced down the front of her body, lingering over her stomach and then moving down to her hip. Clint stood mesmerized by the sight of her as she writhed against the tree and freely explored her own body as though he wasn't even there.

Bending at the knees, Jillian squatted down so she could get a hold of her skirts and began pulling them up slowly. First, the knee-high boots she wore became visible and then Clint got a nice, delicious view of the creamy white skin of her thighs. Jillian's undergarments were already pushed aside and when her hands got that far, she pulled them down, wriggling her body until they were bunched up on the ground at her foot.

Once again, Clint had to restrain himself. His penis ached to be inside of her. When he saw the small thatch of dark hair between her legs, he instinctively began removing his pants and stepping closer.

"No," Jillian groaned. ". . . watch . . ."

With her eyes still closed and her head leaning back, she moved the tip of her finger up and down over the pink lips of her vagina, changing to small, fast circles when she reached the more sensitive skin above them. Jillian kept her skirt hiked up around her waist so her hands were free to move between her legs. Opening her eyes, she looked at Clint hungrily, slipping the tip of her finger inside herself. When she pushed in a little farther, she groaned softly and smiled, biting sensuously into her lower lip.

Clint couldn't wait any longer. Stepping forward, he slid his hands beneath her skirts and felt the soft curve of her hips. He leaned forward, opened his mouth and ran his tongue over her lips, until she kissed him deeply. Soon, he felt her hand wrapping around his rigid cock, stroking it slowly while guiding it in between her legs.

"Tell me what's gonna happen to me," she whispered.

"We're going to make love all night long and then try not to let your father catch on when he's got a pick in his hand."

Jillian laughed again. Only this time, it was genuine and free of any other emotion except for pure joy. The sound caught in her throat as Clint pushed deeper inside of her, causing her to arch her back and press her head against the tree. Clint kissed up and down her neck as he slid in and out of her, savoring the taste of her skin every bit as much as the way her hair tickled the back of his neck.

Once again, Jillian moved her fingers between her legs, feeling the soft lips there and gently rubbing over Clint's shaft as it pumped inside and back out again. She brought her hand up and touched the moistness on her finger against Clint's mouth. Reflexively, his tongue darted out to get a taste of her juices. In the next second, she kissed him hard on the lips, their tongues mingling together to enjoy the pure taste of one another.

When their lips parted, Jillian leaned her head forward to rest it on Clint's shoulder. Her arms reached around to clasp tightly around him while she raised up one of her legs to wrap it around his waist.

Clint could feel the muscles of her leg tightening around him, the sensation feeling slightly different than what he was used to simply because they were standing up. Still, he had no trouble supporting her weight and even reached down to hold the leg she'd raised, which allowed him to penetrate even deeper inside of her. Burying his penis in between her thighs until their bodies came together, Clint reached down with both hands, grabbed onto her tightly clenched bottom, and lifted her up off her feet so she could wrap both legs around him.

Struggling to keep her voice down, Jillian whispered, "Yes, Clint, yes. Push it into me."

Making sure her back was firmly against the tree, he pounded into her with enough force to shake the branches above his head. With every thrust, Jillian bit into her lip a little harder, clawed at his back a little deeper, and clenched her eyes shut a little tighter. Finally, Clint could feel her pussy constricting around him, gripping his cock with the quick spasms of her orgasm as it pulsed through every part of her body.

When the waves subsided, Jillian unlocked her legs and dropped her feet back down to the ground. She then took a step back and slipped Clint out of her, making sure that her hand was still rubbing up and down his shaft as he came out. Before Clint could say anything, Jillian had dropped down to her knees in front of him and wrapped her lips around the head of his penis.

She sucked on him while both hands reached around to grab the backs of his legs, devouring him like he was her last meal. Parting her soft, full lips, she devoured every inch of him, running her tongue up underneath his length. Jillian bobbed her head back and forth, clenching her lips tightly around him until she could feel Clint's hands reach down and hold the back of her head.

Once again, this time with him in her mouth, the corners of her mouth curled up into a naughty smirk. As soon as she lightly ran the ends of her fingernails down his legs, Jillian took all of his cock into her mouth and massaged him with her tongue.

Clint fought to keep from groaning loudly as he exploded into her mouth. Jillian kept her lips locked around him until his muscles finally relaxed and he let out the breath he'd been holding. Getting back to her feet, she rubbed her body against Clint's and held him for the next few minutes, listening to his heartbeat racing in the dark.

They drifted back to camp, hand in hand, walking quietly back to the warm circle of firelight. Clint was glad to hear the loud, grating snores coming from where Eldon was curled up beside the wagon.

THIRTY-TWO

Clint slept through the night with one eye open. His walk through the woods with Jillian earlier had almost been enough to put him right to sleep as soon as he got back to camp. However, it didn't take long for his responsibilities to come rushing back at him, reminding him that he was there to make sure that the Grearys lived long enough to see the next evening.

Sitting in the spot he'd picked out when they'd first arrived, Clint rested as much as he could without losing consciousness, listening to the subtle sounds of the night. He could also hear Jillian's breathing become heavier as she eventually drifted off into a contented sleep.

As he'd suspected, the night passed without so much as a peep from Hardam or his men. Even though Clint would have bet that that was going to be the way it worked out, he wasn't about to gamble Eldon's and Jillian's lives on it. When the first hint of sunlight peeked up over the horizon and reached in through the trees, Clint felt his eyelids turn into lead hoods. The sunlight seemed to shine directly into his face, and the first sounds made by Eldon as he stirred awake pounded against Clint's weary eardrums, causing him to lower his head like a wounded animal.

Clint didn't even get a chance to grieve properly for the pains in his sore muscles before Eldon was whistling a happy tune and fixing a cooking fire. When the sun made its full presence known, the smell of fresh coffee and bacon was drifting through the air. Finally, Clint had found a reason to live.

"Mornin'," Eldon said when Clint turned around and shuffled over to the fire. "You look like you had a rough night."

For a second, Clint felt like a guilty teenager who'd slept with the farmer's daughter. But then he realized that he and Eldon weren't on the same track, so Clint simply nodded and tried to work out the kinks in his joints. "Yeah. Thought I'd make sure that nobody tried to creep up on us during the night."

"Well, ya did a good enough job. Looks like we're all fine and ready to go. Hope you got a bit of sleep, though."

"I think I nodded off a few times, but not enough to keep from waking up whenever a leaf hit the ground. I'll take some of that coffee, if you don't mind."

Eldon poured a generous portion of the steaming brew into a mug and handed it over to Clint. "Best try to get as much energy as you can. We got a *long* day ahead of us."

"Leave him alone, Father," came Jillian's voice from the other side of the camp. "At least let the man wake up before you start driving him like that poor mule of yours."

Clint sipped his coffee and did his best to try and shake the cobwebs from his head that had been gathered during a sleepless night on guard duty. Breakfast consisted of bacon and corn meal served with a side of warm baked beans. The only thing that brightened Clint's morning was seeing Jillian tend to the camp and give him knowing looks whenever Eldon was looking in another direction.

Her hair was a rumpled mess after sleeping on it and there was even a bit of tree bark caught amid her light brown curls. Seeing that brought a smile to Clint's face and when he pointed it out to her, Jillian turned the shade of the bright red dawn.

In less than an hour, breakfast was over and the camp was packed up into the back of the wagon. Eldon scurried about the place like an excited child, barking out orders and prodding the others along until they were moving just as fast as he was.

"C'mon," Eldon hollered. "The quicker we get to that mine, the quicker we can get out!"

Clint let out an aggravated grumble. "Maybe we should hook you up to the wagon and you could pull us all up those cliffs. Hell, I bet we'd get there in half the time."

Laughing, Jillian said, "He does get excited when he gets near the mines. He always told me he could feel the gold just waiting for him to dig it up. It's even worse if we're going to a spot where he's already made a strike."

"It could also be that coffee he made," Clint said with a shudder. "It makes me feel like my blood's being pumped through me by a steam engine."

"Now you see why I usually do most of the cooking."

"Too bad we couldn't get Hardam to drink a few cups. Maybe then he'd keel over and we wouldn't even have to worry about him."

Eldon was too busy getting the wagon ready to roll to pay any attention to the jokes being made at his expense. Instead, he snapped the reins for his mule and sent the wagon rolling toward a path that wound its way up into the cliffs. He bore every bump in the path with a smile and regarded every rock that slipped beneath the mule's hooves as a good sign.

At one point, the wagon nearly slid off the trail completely, but Eldon handled it like a professional and even said that it was good to find such things on the way up since coming down was so much more dangerous. At least now they knew where to look when they were weighed down on their return trip.

All the while, Clint kept to the back of the line with his eyes and ears absorbing every little thing. He knew the real trouble would begin as soon as they got to the mine. But that shouldn't be for at least another . . .

"All right, Mister Adams," Eldon shouted excitedly. "We're here."

THIRTY-THREE

The mine didn't have a name.

There was a couple of small boards nailed to the leaning framework holding up the entrance, but any lettering that might have been on it at one time was long since gone. Eldon stood at the entrance as though it was the gate to heaven, a reverent tilt to his head and a smile that grew wider whenever he so much as looked inside the dark, yawning tunnel.

"This is it," Eldon said with a vague sense of majesty in his tone.

Clint hadn't been to a lot of mines, but this one even looked dangerous to him. When he touched the wooden frame supporting the entrance, the timber shifted slightly, causing a small flow of dust and powder to rain down onto the top of his hat.

"If Hardam wants us dead," Clint pointed out, "he might not have to do a whole lot of work if we all go in this thing."

"She's safe enough, Mister Adams," Eldon said proudly. "I been in here so many times I barely even need the map."

"How far in do you have to go for the gold?"

"There's a vein that starts in one of the lower tunnels. I'll get right to it and Jillian will help me carry up the first load."

Clint's eyes snapped over to Jillian who was already tending to the torches and making sure that their equipment was ready to go. She didn't seemed at all concerned with the thought of entering the treacherous-looking mine. In fact, she was only slightly less excited than her father.

Looking up from what she was doing, Jillian smiled at Clint and handed over one of the lanterns she'd just filled to Eldon. "Before you say anything, Clint, just let me tell you that I've been doing this since I could walk. There's no need to worry about either one of us. We'll be fine."

Before Clint could say another word, Eldon was suited up with thick gloves covering his hands and a coil of rope winding over his shoulder. The rest of him was covered with a thick coat that looked as though it had been sunken at the bottom of a river before being dragged behind a team of wild horses. He slung a pickax over one shoulder and a shovel over the other. Next to him, Jillian grabbed hold of a pair of lanterns and a sack half full of various supplies.

Jillian handed another lantern to her father and let him go on inside ahead of her. She then leaned in close to Clint and put her lips close enough to his ear that he could just barely feel them flutter against his skin when she spoke.

"Watch out for me," she whispered. "Make sure nothing bad happens . . . at least until I get back and we can be alone again."

Kissing her once on the cheek, Clint held her at arm's length and looked into her eyes. "If you hear any commotion out here, I want you and Eldon to stay hidden inside that mine. Something tells me that Hardam won't be able to find you in there with an army of men."

Jillian nodded. "I'll tell Father. He'll want to help you, though."

"The most helpful thing he could do is stay down in that mine until I call for him. That way, I won't have to worry about either of you if the lead starts to fly."

A worried shadow drifted across Jillian's face just then, which was exactly what Clint wanted. Now was the time to be worried . . . and very, very careful.

Nodding, Jillian said, "He'll be too busy digging to worry about much more than that anyway. But you promise me to take care of yourself." She stepped up close to him and ran her fingers through his hair before gently kissing his ear. "I don't care how much gold is down there," she whispered. "There isn't enough to replace a man like you."

Clint restrained himself from saying anything more. Instead, he took a long look at her and turned away, listening to the sound of her footsteps as she entered the cave to track down Eldon.

The mine swallowed up every last trace of the Grearys almost immediately. Soon, Clint couldn't see a hint of light from their lanterns and couldn't hear even the scratch of a single step. He supposed that was a good thing since that meant that there wasn't any trouble. He wasn't worried about Hardam beating them to the mine and waiting to spring a trap. After all, if the man knew where the mine was, there'd be no reason for him to track Eldon or even fight him. Hardam would simply steal the gold and deal with the consequences later.

The sad part was that there probably wouldn't have been any consequences. Now, with the conflict underway and Clint on the job, there would most definitely be consequences when Hardam eventually made his move. Dire consequences.

The entrance to the mine was on a wide shelf of rock roughly a hundred feet above the ground. There was enough space for the wagon, the animals and Clint himself to all sit comfortably and wait for word from inside the tunnels. And wait they did . . . for no less than three hours straight without so much as a peep from the cold, black depths of the mine.

Clint led Eclipse up the trail a ways, took the rifle from its saddle holster and tied him off at a spot Eldon had told him about, and then made his way back to the mine's entrance. He kept himself busy fashioning a place for himself to sit using a few old crates that had been left over from the last time Eldon had been up this way.

From his perch above the trees, he couldn't see much besides the canopy of leaves swaying like a vast green ocean with every passing breeze. It even sounded like water flowing when the wind picked up enough, but when Clint tried to breathe in deeply to fill his lungs with the fresh smell, all he got was a lung full of dust to remind him of where he really was.

It was going to be a hot day. Hell, it already *was* a hot day. And the more he thought about it, the hotter it got. Clint adjusted his hat to block out as much of the sun as possible and leaned back against the cool stone. That was when he heard something else besides the dry wind and whisper of leaves brushing against one another.

It was a sound that was just loud enough for him to catch. If not for the direction of the wind and the echoing effect of the cliff face itself, he more than likely would have missed it completely. But he could hear it all right . . . just barely.

The steady drumming of horses making their way across solidly packed land.

Clint jumped up from his seat and made his way to the edge of the rock shelf. Looking down on the trees, he studied the foliage carefully until he found what he was looking for.

Clint had almost forgotten about the traps he'd set outside the camp's perimeter, designed to attract his attention. That was what had alerted him to their presence.

There . . . he could see them now . . . making their way through the campsite that Clint and the Grearys had slept in the night before . . . a line of horsemen with a small wagon trailing behind. But there were too many of them to just be Hardam's men. From what he could see, Clint counted at least half a dozen men plus whatever was in that wagon.

Now that he knew they were there, Clint only had to figure out one thing: what on earth he could do about it.

THIRTY-FOUR

The horsemen rolled through the campsite, not even pausing long enough to look for what had been left behind. They kept moving, heading straight for the trail that would lead them up to the mine. Clint watched, the pit of his stomach clenching as two of the horsemen separated from the rest to stay with the wagon while the others began ascending the cliffs.

Clint made his way back to the edge of the shelf, making sure to keep his head down by moving in a low crouch. Once he got to the edge, he knelt down and brought the rifle up to his shoulder, just in case the horsemen were simply waiting for a target to show itself.

When no shots came, Clint leaned a little farther out, trying to get a look at the trail that wound its way up to the mine's entrance. He couldn't see anyone approaching just yet, but that didn't mean they weren't coming. Clint knew from experience that the lower portion of the trail worked its way around another side of the cliff before winding back around to his current position.

If the horsemen were still taking their time, that left Clint with an hour or two before they would be in sight. If they hurried, they might just do him a favor by slipping right off the side of the cliff. But Clint knew enough about Hardam to know that the man wouldn't come this far and risk this much just to lose everything to a stupid mistake.

Clint lowered himself down so that he was laying on his belly looking out over the edge. Just to be prepared, he sighted down the rifle wherever he looked, knowing full well that the first shots could come at any time. For the moment, he was more concerned with the men that were still down below with that wagon.

If the wagon had been brought just to haul gold, then they would have probably brought it up with them. And if it was just going to wait down there to be filled later, then why leave two guards to sit with it when Hardam knew what kind of opposition he'd be facing? That only left one other possibility: that the wagon was either carrying something valuable or something that needed men to guard it.

Clint sat in position, watching what little movement he could see through the trees until the sound of approaching hooves began filtering to his ears. He didn't have to look to know who was coming and where they were coming from, which was at least something of an advantage. The only thing he didn't know was what was in that wagon. And the more Clint thought about that particular question, the more it got under his skin.

Finally, once the approaching horsemen got close enough, Clint got to his feet and put his back to the cliff face. He waited there with his rifle in hand, knowing that Hardam would be expecting him to go for the Colt first off. At this point, whatever little thing he could stack in his favor would have to do. That was the only way to beat odds stacked this badly against him.

The first horse to come around the corner was Hardam's. The rider looked more like a gambler than a robber, decked out in a black overcoat and string tie. As soon as he spotted Clint, Hardam put on the wide, conniving smile of a man who was certain he had accounted for every possible angle.

Hardam brought his horse to a stop and held up his open hand to signal for the men behind him to do the same. Clint noticed that he did, indeed, stop just out of regular pistol range. Too bad Clint's Colt had been modified to something well past regular.

"Still working for the old man, Adams?" Hardam asked with a taunting sneer.

Clint locked eyes with the leader of the horsemen and brought the rifle up to his shoulder. "Still trying to run down men who can't fight against you?"

Although Hardam's eyes widened a bit when he saw the rifle pointed at him, it wasn't enough to put a dent in his confidence. "We owe you something for killing Anderson. That kid was no match for you. Hell, that was such an unfair fight it should be considered murder."

"Then why'd you send him after me? The way I remember it, I was the one attacked. Anderson had every chance to move along."

Two men drew up next to Hardam. One was the man who'd been with him outside of the saloon when the boy had died and the other didn't look familiar at all. He had the cold, focused eyes of a killer, which locked onto Clint as though he was already lining up his shot.

"I know who you are, Gunsmith," Hardam continued. "And I respect you. That's why I'm giving you one chance to clear on out of here before I start in on that old man and his mine. Did you get a chance to look at what I got down there?" he asked, nodding in the direction of the ledge that Clint had been lying on. "Why not take a look?"

Clint edged along the wall, being sure to keep the rock to his back and the horsemen in sight. None of the men seemed to be making a move, so when he got close enough to look over the side, Clint did so quickly. One glance was all he needed.

The first things he saw were stacks of boxes in the back of the wagon. The two men who'd been guarding the wagon had since moved in behind it and were busy making adjustments to the two large metallic objects. A second peek confirmed his suspicions, turning the uneasy feeling in Clint's stomach to a full-grown knot.

Before saying another word, Clint moved back away from the ledge, reflexively keeping his head low. "What the hell do you think you're gonna do with those detonators?" Clint asked, his anger boiling up and spilling into the question.

"Are you so crazy that outnumbering us two to one wasn't enough?" Narrowing his eyes, Clint dropped his voice to a rumbling growl. "Or are you just too scared to take on me, an old man and a woman without blowing this whole damn place sky-high?"

Hardam was enjoying himself too much to be affected by Clint's words. Instead, he smiled broadly and shook his head. "Provoking me isn't going to get you anything but dead. I do, however, think you should know that I've got more explosives than what you see here and I'm prepared to bury you and the Greary family down in there so deep that even God won't know where to look for the bodies.

"So you've got one more chance to make up your mind. You can walk away, or I'll call down so much hell that you couldn't possibly survive. It's your decision, Adams. Make it quickly."

THIRTY-FIVE

Hardam sat atop his horse like a king glaring down from his castle. The men to either side of him looked only too eager to start shooting, and Clint could almost feel that same kind of anxiousness coming from the men at that wagon. They were all waiting for their moment to strike.

Just then, Clint was certain of one thing: Whatever answer he gave to Hardam, the result would be the same. They were going to try and kill him and the Grearys and then take their gold, no matter what. That was why they'd come.

With that fact locked firmly in mind, Clint tightened his grip around the rifle, fixed his eyes solidly onto Hardam and gave the only answer he could think of.

"Fuck you," Clint snarled.

Hardam glared back at him as though he hadn't expected anything less. With a wave of his hand, he motioned for the others. "Then let's get this over with. Kill them all."

Both of the men who'd been next to Hardam went for their guns while snapping their reins to send their horses forward. As soon as the way was cleared, another rider shot forward with both hands filled with pistols. Bosner swung down from his saddle and yanked his shotgun free from its holster as Jervis slid down to the ground to land on his feet like a cat after jumping from a tree's lowest branch.

Clint dropped to one knee and prepared to fire at the man

closest to him, which would have been Bosner. But then, a
rider he hadn't even seen before came storming past all the
rest, eager to be the first to pull his trigger.

The man making his charge peeled his lips back into a
crazy smile as a battle cry tore out from the depths of his
stomach. Before he could bring both guns around to bear on
his target, he was knocked straight back out of his saddle by
a round from Clint's rifle. The bullet hit him square in the
chest and lifted him up off the back of his horse, allowing
the animal to keep right on running to the opposite end of
the ledge.

Clint took another step into the mine, struggling to look
around the charging horse so he could see where the next
shot was coming from. By the time the animal had passed,
Hardam was riding behind Eldon's wagon while the other
two dove for cover on foot.

Always thinking on the best way to waste human life,
Hardam had used the first gunman as a distraction. Now that
his job was done, the wounded man was left sitting alone in
the open, blood pouring from the gaping hole in his chest.
His mouth opened and closed with no sound coming out. His
arm tried in vain to bring up his gun and then the disap-
pointment showed on his face when the strength to do such
a simple thing wasn't there.

His life drained out of him . . .

. . . and nobody noticed.

The bullets started flying through the air like misdirected
hail. Bits of lead whipped past Clint's face, coming within
inches of ending his life, only to spark against the rock behind him. All the air exploded as guns went off and powder
burned and more shots came toward him until it was all Clint
could do to keep his wits from leaving him completely.

It was more instinct than anything else that kept him focused on only what was needed. The first thing he had to do
was get behind some cover or eventually one of those rounds
was going to bury itself deep into his flesh. Clint threw himself to one side, landing on his ribs and pulling himself

around to the entrance of the mine where he could take a
breath and assess his situation.

Even though he'd been expecting things to go badly as
soon as Hardam arrived, there was no way for him to prepare
for what actually came. Now, besides factoring in the extra
men, he had to figure out how to handle the artillery that
Hardam had somehow gotten his hands on.

When the shots died down a little, Clint poked his head
around the side and fired off a few rounds in Hardam's general direction. They went high, but they caused Bosner and
the other strange face to stop where they were and drop down
to the ground. Already, the gunmen were beginning to close
in on the mine. It wouldn't be long before they got even
more brave and tried to rush him.

Clint was beginning to regret this whole thing. Most of
all, he regretted the way he'd figured Hardam would come
at him. Taking a few more shots with the rifle, Clint swore
to himself and shoved a couple more cartridges into the
breach.

The angle of the sun was in his favor, shining down over
the cliffs and right into the eyes of Hardam and his men.
Clint took advantage of this by pressing his back against the
wall of the tunnel and sliding inside the shadow so he could
get a longer look at what was going on outside without being
immediately spotted.

By this time, the firing had stopped. Clint watched from
his hiding place as Bosner motioned over his shoulder and
the stranger got up to walk calmly over to Eldon's wagon.
They spoke quietly among themselves before the stranger
and yet another gunman Clint hadn't seen before walked over
to the mule and untied it from the wagon. Once it was free,
one of the new men started going through the contents of
the wagon, tossing them out all over the rock.

Meanwhile, Hardam finally got off his horse and spoke to
Bosner, gesturing toward the mine. He called out to the first
stranger, who reached inside his coat and pulled out something as thick as Clint's arm that resembled several candle-
sticks wrapped together by black twine.

Hardam took a moment to attach a fuse and then looked

back toward the mine. This time, he looked directly at Clint
. . . and winked.

It was at that moment that Clint realized just how crazy
Hardam was.

The hiss of the fuse being lit sounded like a giant snake
to Clint's ears. If he was lucky, he had about ten seconds
before it blew, sending the entire top portion of the cliffs
down on top of him and those he'd sworn to protect.

THIRTY-SIX

Hardam still held the match in hand that he'd just used to light the fuse of the dynamite in the stranger's fist. Watching the sparking string sputter and hiss as it crept closer to the explosives, Hardam brought the match up to his face and touched it to a cigarette that dangled from his lips. Smiling, he took a leisurely breath full of smoke and plucked the dynamite away from the stranger.

"Now this," Hardam said as he hefted the explosives and tossed them toward the entrance to the mine, "is the way to deal with a problem."

All at once, every man standing near the mine bolted for cover, scattering like panicked quail when they saw that there was no real shelter to be found. Hardam, on the other hand, strolled around the wagon and dropped down to a sitting position. He took the cigarette from his month and held it in front of him, admiring the glowing embers, anticipating the destruction that was only seconds away.

Bosner threw himself facefirst beneath the wagon and covered the back of his head with his hands.

Jervis and one of Rattler's other men jogged down the path that had brought them up the side of the cliff until there was enough of the rockface between themselves and the open tunnel.

They all got to their positions . . . and waited for the fire-ball that would mark the end of Clint Adams.

Clint's first impulse was to run down into the mines where he could get the most protection from the blast. The only problem with that idea, of course, was that he and everyone else would have been buried inside the rock for the rest of their natural lives. Then Clint heard the hissing fuse as it spun through the air, landing with a solid *thunk* as the package of explosives dropped squarely at the mouth of the mine.

There was enough dynamite to blow every part of his body half a mile in different directions. And there was enough fuse to give him about a second and a half to prevent that from happening.

Before he knew what he was doing, Clint was scrambling in the exact opposite direction than what his instincts told him to go. He threw himself toward the dynamite and grabbed hold of the package with one hand. Using the other, he reached out, grabbed the fuse and plucked it free from the stick.

Reflexively, Clint's eyes clenched shut in expectation of oblivion.

What he got instead was the sharp, burning pain as the fuse burned right down to his fingers before being snuffed out.

Clint tucked the dynamite underneath his arm and took off down the tunnel before the gunmen decided to come in and check to see what happened to the explosion they'd been waiting for. He made it about twenty feet before he realized that he'd forgotten one very important thing: Light.

Once he got far enough inside the mine that he was out of reach of the sun's illumination, Clint might as well have been running with his eyes closed. He stopped, held his hand out and began slowly turning around toward the direction he'd entered. Behind him, there were the sounds of rushing footsteps and angry voices.

Hardam's men came looking for their target and all they got was an empty tunnel.

• • •

Hardam stood outside the mine for a second, just to make sure that he hadn't simply misjudged the length of the fuse. Once he was certain there was going to be no explosion, he bolted inside the mine and looked angrily at the faces of Bosner and Jervis.

Looking to Bosner, Hardam felt the anger inside of him flush through his body and turn his skin a shade of deep crimson. "What's the matter?" he asked. "Can't you even put together a few sticks of dynamite without having it fall apart?"

"You'd better thank god that that stuff didn't go off," Bosner replied. "Because all it would've left you was a smoking pile of rocks. No gold. No money. No nothing. And who did you say the idiot was?"

Jervis scanned the area without saying a word. He walked around Bosner and Hardam so he could reach down and pick something up off of the ground. He held up the singed remains of the fuse and shoved it in between the faces of the two men. "After all you hear about Adams, you think you can just toss something at him and blow him up?"

Both Hardam and Bosner stopped what they were saying and looked over to Jervis. As much as they wanted to keep on arguing their points, they couldn't think of anything good enough to say after hearing Jervis's statement. Hardam clenched his teeth and wrangled control of himself away from his rage while Bosner simply threw up his arms and stormed off toward the darkness.

"All right then," Hardam said evenly. "What do you propose we do about Adams?"

The well-dressed killer tossed the fuse to the ground and carefully wiped his fingertips on a handkerchief he fished from his pocket. "We've got to keep on trying to overpower him since we don't have a prayer of being faster than him."

"And I thought you were supposed to be fast," Hardam prodded.

"Speed is one thing. Intelligence is another. Without one, the other is useless and right now, we need to rely on intelligence. Adams is a cornered animal right now. All we have to do is wait him out and he'll trip up. After that . . . the rest is easy."

Bosner stepped into the alcove where Clint had been hiding. He stopped there and sniffed the air as though he could still smell the lingering evidence of Clint's presence. As much as he strained his eyes, he simply could not see past another couple of feet before the tunnel and everything inside of it disappeared. Even other shadows were swallowed up by the void, sending chills up and down his spine.

Suddenly, there was a subtle movement at the spot where the last remaining rays of the sun met to form a pool of gray right before the blackness took over. The movement wasn't much . . . just enough to catch Bosner's attention. It was all he needed to bring his weapon up and aim toward the other end of the tunnel. "Hey, shut up, both of you," Bosner snarled. "There's somebody coming."

Almost immediately, Hardam's and Jervis's guns were pointed toward the shadows. Within the space of a second, those two had spotted the shifting motions as well.

Hardam's anger was forgotten when he saw the figure coming toward him. Without taking his eyes away from the movement, he said to Bosner, "Go signal for Welles to bring up the rest of the dynamite. It's time to take care of the infestation problem we have in these tunnels."

Taking his time, Hardam brought up his .45 and sighted carefully down the barrel while applying just enough pressure on the trigger to move the hammer. He was ready to fire, but only waited until he could see the face of his prey. He saw the face he'd been looking for . . . and got ready to blow it clean of its skull.

THIRTY-SEVEN

Clint froze in the darkness.

He pressed his back against the wall, looking from side to side as though his eyes would do him any good. In front of him, there was just the tunnel leading to the entrance, which was now crowded with Hardam and his men. Behind, there was a cold, inky tunnel, which yawned quietly like the mouth of a sleeping giant.

Clint knew he could take his chances with the dark and feel his way slowly to a nearby corner where he could be safe from the bullets that were only seconds away from coming. He could also walk straight into a gunfight where he was outnumbered four to one.

Either way he cut it, Clint didn't much care for his odds.

The rifle felt good and solid in his hands, like the only concrete thing that was left in his world. He might not be able to see it, but he knew it was there and that it could help him. Right now, that was more than he could say even for the ground beneath his feet. Bringing the rifle up to his shoulder, Clint decided to go with the one sure thing he had left and see how far that rifle could take him.

Just as he was about to squeeze the trigger, he sensed something coming up behind him. It wasn't anything more than a bad feeling that drifted over his skin like fingernails scraping gently across his flesh, but the feeling was there nonetheless. Swiveling around in one quick motion, Clint brought the rifle to bear on a piece of the darkness that somehow separated itself from the rest. It was a man-sized piece only slightly shorter than himself. Just above where its forehead should have been, there was the faintest glimmer of reflected light.

"Hold on," came a familiar, insistent voice. "Don't shoot."

Clint squinted at the shadow, but was unable to make anything more out of it than a vague shape. "Is that you, Eldon?"

"Sure enough. Now point that weapon at someone that deserves it."

Once again, the bad feeling swept through Clint's body, only this time it caused him to drop reflexively to one knee. Just as his hand reached up to grab hold of Eldon and drag him down as well, Clint heard a single shot echo off the walls and thunder down into the tunnel, making it impossible for Clint to hear much else for a couple of seconds.

Clint reached out for Eldon and closed his fist on nothing but empty air.

"Eldon?" Clint whispered to the space where the old man had just been.

There was no reply.

Just the sound of ragged, painful breaths.

Clint moved his hand down lower and immediately touched something warm and wet. The texture on his fingers was thick and viscous. "Oh, no," he said as he gently felt for where Eldon had fallen. He found him right away, laying in a heap against the wall directly behind him.

Trying not to do any more damage than what had already been done, Clint took his hand away from where Eldon was laying and scooted in a little closer to the old man. "Eldon, where did they get you?"

At first, there was no response except for some strained breathing and a few painful grunts.

Clint shifted his attention from where the bullet had landed to where it had come from. Back toward the end of the tunnel, Hardam and his men had begun making their way into the shadows. Although it was hard for Clint to see much of anything, he could hear their steps and voices echoing off the bare stone walls as though each sound was amplified ten times over.

"I hit him!" Bosner shouted. "I can't see much, but I know for damn sure that I hit the son of a bitch."

Hardam was the one itching to go charging into the shadows, but he hesitated once he realized that he wouldn't be able to see anything until he'd tripped over it. Turning to look over his shoulder, he said, "Somebody get me one of them lanterns. I can't see shit in here."

Clint stayed absolutely still. He could sense the others' eyes on him, but after a few seconds of squinting, they cursed under their breath and remained where they were. As they bickered among themselves about who should be the one to fetch some light, Clint slowly brought his gun up and pointed it toward the group of men.

He knew he'd only be able to get off one shot, maybe two, before the rest of the gunmen filled the tunnel with flying lead. While shifting the weapon to point the right way, Clint became aware that something as little as a stray beam of light catching some of the steel gun barrel might give away the fact that someone was alive and moving directly in front of them.

The rifle slid over Clint's body as his hands got ready to lever in a fresh round and shoot in one fluid motion. The only reason he didn't go for the Colt at his side was because that would require even more movement before he got to take his shot.

Suddenly, Eldon let out a loud cry of pain as his body began to convulse on the ground next to Clint.

The sound was like a dinner bell to a bunch of hungry scavengers as the faces of Hardam and the others lit up with perverted glee, pushing all other concerns to the side.

"I'll get the lantern," Jervis said. "Just don't let him move from that spot."

Bosner and Hardam crept closer to the source of the sound, suddenly feeling their bravery flow back into them with the knowledge that their target had one foot in the grave already.

A cold certainty settled over Clint at that moment. He knew that if he didn't get Eldon up and away from these killers, than he might as well put a bullet in the old man's head just to save him from whatever Hardam had in store. He snaked his arm along the wall until he found the old man's shoulder and slid around to grab hold of him tightly.

"You ready?" Clint whispered.

Eldon's muscles spasmed when Clint moved him, but he put his arm around Clint's neck and tried to help as much as he could. "Y-yeah. I'll d-d-do my best."

Hardam's eyes glimmered in the near-darkness like a rat's. When Bosner tried to say something to him, he silenced the other man with a quick wave of his hand. The sounds of movement were getting louder. Just loud enough, in fact, for him to pinpoint exactly where they were coming from.

"It's all over, Adams," Hardam said as he held his pistol out and aimed toward the scuffling. "Come on over here and we can watch you while we take the gold. It's all we want. After that . . . we'll leave. I ain't got no feud with you."

Stepping up next to Hardam, Bosner walked a little quicker toward the spot he'd fired upon, eyes searching for that movement in the shadows that he'd seen before.

Clint made sure he had a good, solid hold on Eldon before getting his feet beneath him. Even though he had no idea about what was farther up ahead in the tunnels, he took a breath and got ready to run.

He'd have one or two free steps before the shooting started. After that, there could be low beams hanging from the ceiling, rubble strewn on the floor, dead ends, pits deep enough to swallow them both, or even swarms of bats, rats or worse.

Pushing all of that out of his mind, Clint took hold of his rifle in one hand and Eldon in the other . . . and bolted into a blind man's nightmare.

THIRTY-EIGHT

Hardam was staring into the darkness, trying to judge Clint Adams's height and build when he heard the sounds of desperate footsteps making a break for freedom. His teeth clenched together at the thought of Bosner not being able to put his target down, and he took aim for himself. Hardam pointed his .45 at the spot that should have been at the same level as Clint's head or shoulders and started firing.

Bosner could still picture the first silhouette he'd put down and raised his gun at that same area, sending a barrage of lead flying down the tunnel.

Both men stood with their feet planted, determined not to let Clint get past them. They fanned their weapons while moving back and forth to create a deadly arc meant to cut down every living thing in its path.

Sparks flew from the walls and smoke drifted into their eyes and nostrils while the constant explosions hammered away at their eardrums. All the while, the pair couldn't have been happier. The bloodlust written across their faces was akin to spiritual bliss. In their minds, they could already see their names turning into legend.

Clint threw himself into the tunnel, letting his and Eldon's momentum carry them both forward. As he'd figured, he made it about one step before hell came chasing after them.

Knowing that Hardam had already smelled blood, Clint figured the man would only be thinking about finishing what his partner had started. That meant going for kill shots rather than more wounds.

As soon as he began moving, Clint slammed his shoulder against the opposite side of the tunnel and crouched down so low that his knees almost hit his chin while he ran. He used his shoulder to guide him along the tunnel as lead slugs ripped through the air only inches above him. More than a few shredded his back and sides like fiery claws, but the pain only got him moving faster and none of the bullets dug too deeply into his skin.

He didn't have time to think of how Eldon was doing. If Clint stopped even to wonder about the old man, they would both be cut down by the gunfire that was getting closer and closer to claiming them both.

Sparks from the ricochets lit up the tunnel in brief flickers of dim light. It wasn't enough to see much more than the shape of the floor or the occasional glimpse of a loose rock, but it kept them from falling flat on their faces.

It seemed as though Clint was running forever.

Knowing that any second might very well be his last, Clint focused solely on each individual step. Every one he took was another step closer to escape. Every foot of the tunnel he covered brought him that much more time. And as long as there was time, there was hope.

Clint's eyes were trained on the tunnel directly ahead of them. The mine shaft had curved enough to give him a few moments free from the gunfire, but Hardam and Bosner were hot on his tail. Their feet pounded against the rock like an oncoming train that was fixing to run them both into the ground.

Although Clint still had his rifle, he knew that the time it took to fire would be time wasted where he should have been running. Besides, in order to turn and fire, he would have to drop Eldon like a sack of flour. For all he knew, that might just kill the wounded old man.

The steps halted for just a second, giving Clint enough time to pull ahead another ten or fifteen feet. When they started again, Clint looked toward Eldon, instinctively checking on the old man even though he couldn't make out anything past the nose on his face.

Something else caught his eye, though. Something that yanked the bottom completely out of his stomach.

Light.

The dull glow of quickly bobbing light coming from the tunnel behind him. Hardam had gotten his hands on a lantern. And when they came charging around the bend in the tunnel, they'd be able to see their target well enough to fill him full of bloody holes.

The darkness had been Clint's only advantage, and in about two seconds would be taken away from him.

Just then, the grating pain in Clint's left shoulder came to a stop. Unfortunately, that had been the shoulder that he'd been dragging along the wall as a guide. In the next second, Clint twisted around to find where the wall had gone.

Then . . . he was falling.

As soon as Jervis brought in the lantern, Hardam snatched it out of his hands and took off into the tunnel. He could still hear the sounds of the great Clint Adams running away like a whipped dog as he approached the place in the tunnel where it curved to the right. Bosner waited for him and as soon as the lantern showed him the way, he ran right alongside his boss.

The lantern's light was just enough to keep them from running into the walls or tripping over the rocks and timber littering the ground. When they turned the corner, both of them brought up their guns and snapped back the hammers when they saw . . . nothing.

Bosner started to say something, but Hardam gave him a look that froze the words before they could clear his throat. Suddenly, footsteps echoed down the tunnel and both men spun around ready to fire as Jervis came charging up behind them.

Hardam held the lantern up and listened for the sound of those footsteps. But the harder he tried to hear them, the more frustrated he got when he realized there was nothing to hear. The light flickered around him, creating a dim globe of illumination that only stretched a couple of feet in each direction.

What little air there was inside the mine howled through the tunnel like an invisible monster. Every scrape the men's feet made against the ground rattled in the empty space, yet still there was nothing to tell them where Adams had gone. It was as though the cliffs had swallowed him up before Hardam's bullets could find him.

"Where the hell is he?" Jervis asked.

Hardam slowly turned toward the gunman and fought to keep himself from blowing a hole through the man's chest right then and there. Instead, he looked around the tunnel for any sign of Adams.

"Wait a second," Bosner said. When he saw that Hardam wasn't listening, he reached out and grabbed hold of the other man's shoulder.

This time, when Hardam spun around, he did bring up his gun as though he was about to fire.

Bosner ignored the pistol in his face and stared Hardam right in the eyes. "He was shot. I know I hit him."

"That doesn't matter now, does it?" Hardam snarled.

Grabbing Hardam's wrist, Bosner lowered the lantern until more of the light spilled onto the floor. "It does if he left a blood trail that'll lead us right to him."

It took a moment for Hardam to rein in his anger. But then, he looked down at the ground.

And there it was.

Staining the ground near Jervis's boots, slick crimson marks mingled with the dust on the ground. Hardam traced his steps back along the curve in the tunnel, knowing that more of the blood Jervis had stepped in would be waiting to lead them the rest of the way.

At first, all he could see were Jervis's dark, wet footprints. But then Hardam came to a part of the tunnel that had previously been hidden in the dark. Situated on the outer edge of the curve they'd just passed was a wide crack in the wall almost as wide as a grown man. At the bottom of the opening was a pile of several rocks and pebbles coming up to just below Hardam's knees. A dark trail of blood led down the tunnel and right over those rocks.

"I've got him," Hardam shouted.

Bosner came over just as Hardam was preparing to make his way toward the crack. He walked right past the lantern and set his foot at the base of the rock pile. When he looked past the fallen stones, Bosner saw a pair of boots. Then he saw another pair.

"You're a dead man," Bosner said right before he saw the cold black eye of Clint's barrel staring back at him.

Next came a blinding flash . . . a quick jolt of pain . . . and then . . . oblivion.

THIRTY-NINE

When Clint had found the crack in the wall, he'd fallen sideways into the fissure while tripping over the rocks piled up at its base. Eldon had gone right over with him as both men slid on their asses until they wound up with their feet in the air and their backs on the ground.

Clint fought back the impulse to struggle to his feet as Hardam and his men had gone by, hoping that they hadn't seen his graceful maneuver and would keep running past the space he'd found. They'd done just that, giving Clint enough time to replace the rifle he'd dropped during the fall with his modified Colt.

After that, he stayed as quiet as he could and waited to see who was going to be the unlucky man to poke his head through that crack. Bosner won that award and his prize was getting his head turned into a canoe by a single round fired from Clint's gun.

Bosner's face still wore the smug, victorious expression he'd had when he'd first seen Clint laying on his back. Even with the addition of another eye in the middle of his forehead, he still managed to keep the look as his skull was emptied onto the wall behind him and he dropped straight back into the adjacent tunnel.

Still keeping his gun ready from the next target to get in his way, Clint got back onto his feet and reached down for

Eldon. Although the light from Hardam's lantern was faint, it was just enough for him to see where the old man was laying. It was also enough for him to see that Eldon was not moving.

"Come on, Eldon," Clint said as he snaked his free hand beneath one of the miner's shoulders. "This isn't a good time to be getting lazy on me. I need your help if I'm gonna move you any farther."

No response.

Also, the light from just outside the fissure was getting brighter.

Instinctively, Clint shifted his aim to the left to anticipate the next man's move that would look in on him from the main tunnel. But whoever was holding the lantern stopped just short of putting himself into the line of fire, giving Clint another couple of seconds to try and get Eldon up off the ground.

The more Clint tried to lift him, the heavier Eldon got. Especially when he knew that Hardam would be making his move at any second. Finally, there was a twitch in Eldon's muscles and slight groan coming from the back of his throat.

"Uuhnnn—le-leave me."

"You're not getting out of this that easy," Clint said insistently. "Now suck it up and get to your feet before you get us both killed."

"Just go . . . find Jillian."

"We'll both find her. Now do your part and stand up. This is the time when you listen to me. Remember? That was the deal."

Clint took his eyes away from the fissure for a split second to take a quick look at Eldon. The old man had been shot just below the neck, possibly in one of his lungs. The bullet might have also nicked his heart, but Clint doubted that since the wound seemed a bit high for that. Also, if that had been the case, Eldon probably would have been dead by now.

He felt terrible for pushing the poor miner the way he'd been doing, but it was either that or leave him to die and Clint didn't even consider the latter as an option.

Eldon grunted loudly one more time, looked up and suddenly looked as though he was about to pass out from a heart attack as he turned white as a ghost and his eyes became round as saucers. He tried to say something, but could only get out a raspy grunt.

Seeing this, Clint could tell that Eldon was looking at something just over his shoulder. Since that was where the fissure was, Clint pointed his gun that way and took a shot without even looking.

The Colt was still smoking as he turned around and took another shot. This time, he could actually see his target, which was the retreating back of a man who was doing his best to get past the crack in the wall without getting killed for his trouble. Whoever the figure was, he was moving too fast for Clint to see much besides a blur of motion, but he took his second shot all the same.

Light from the lantern trickled into the fissure from the same spot as it had been before. That told Clint that whoever had dived across the opening wasn't the one holding the lantern.

"Hardam," Clint shouted as he finally got to his feet. "How many more of your men are you gonna throw at me before you decide just to come at me on your own? How many more do I have to kill before you get the guts to do your own dirty work? Answer me, goddammit!"

Clint's voice rumbled backward and forward through the mine, gaining power and momentum the more it bounced off the walls and churned through the dark. He kept his eye on that light, knowing that when it moved, so did Hardam. Although it flickered and wavered a bit every now and again, the source hadn't yet budged.

Unsure of whether it was his own strength or a final burst from Eldon, Clint felt the old man get a bit lighter in his grasp and with another pull, was once again standing beside him on his own two feet. Eldon held on tightly to Clint and urged him to walk farther down into the fissure.

As he backed up, Clint still watched that light. Part of him didn't want to leave it out of spite for Hardam, while the other part didn't want to leave without getting the damn lantern for his own use. But Eldon was insistent enough to get them both moving and Clint turned to watch where he was going while there was still enough light to watch anything at all.

"Come and get me, you yellow bastard!" Clint hollered as he moved farther away from the light. "Come to me so we can finish this!"

Hardam stood with his back pressed up against the wall right next to the large, jagged crack. He stared across at the gruesome stucco of bone fragments and brain matter stuck to the opposite wall. Bosner's corpse lay in a heap on the ground, his eyes still wide open as though he was watching Clint get away.

A bloody mist still hung in the air, clouding Hardam's vision. That had been put there when Jervis tried rushing into the crevice, only to get a bullet for his troubles. Although the other man was still moving, Hardam wasn't sure if he was running or falling at this point.

Clint's voice rang through the mine, masking the sound of his footsteps, and when Hardam tried to catch a glimpse around the corner, the red mist moved along the walls like a living thing. He held up the lantern and saw the speckles of blood that had been sprayed across the glass cover. It could have been Bosner's or even Jervis's, but it was most definitely a warning that spoke directly to the survival instinct in Hardam's brain.

He stayed where he was, pressed against the wall, listening to the taunting of his enemy, plotting how he was going to make sure that Clint Adams never left that mine alive.

FORTY

The anger boiling inside of Clint's chest faded away just as quickly as the light inside the mine. As he and Eldon got farther along down the narrow passage, Clint's attention focused less on Hardam and more on simply finding his way through the dark without taking another fall like the one that had brought him into this cramped fissure.

Unlike the one they'd left behind, this passage felt rougher and more natural. Less like a mine and more like something that had been inside the rocks ever since the cliff had been formed. Joining the sounds of their boots scraping against the rock, there were also sounds of smaller feet scrambling back and forth and all around . . .

. . . everywhere . . .

. . . hundreds of them . . .

"You still with me, Eldon?" Clint asked. He wasn't so much looking for an answer as he was trying to give himself something else to listen to besides the clicking of tiny nails along the floor and walls.

The old man's voice sounded rough, but surprisingly strong. "There ain't a lot of places for me to go at the moment, but I'm movin' . . . thanks to you."

"Well, don't thank me yet. I got a few of Hardam's men, but he's still out there and I know he's got reinforcements.

Also, we could be walking into another fall right now because I can't see a damn thing."

"Don't . . . don't worry about that," Eldon grunted as pain stabbed through his body. "I know exactly where we are. This is . . . the way I took to meet up with you to begin with."

Clint tried to ignore the sound of scuttling vermin all around him. He also tried not to think about how badly Eldon was hurt. What he needed was to get the old man to safety before he could let anything else creep into his mind. After all, no matter how badly Eldon's wound was, it wouldn't make a bit of difference if Hardam's killers got to them first.

The sound of their footsteps eventually got softer as more and more silt or dirt covered the tunnel's floor. Also, Clint began feeling tiny legs scurrying across his feet. Sometimes they would grab hold of his pants leg and try to work their way up. But Clint shook the rodents off as he moved, focusing his attention on the bits of the tunnel that he could see.

"My eyes must be getting used to the dark," Clint said after a few minutes of walking. "I think I can make out a junction up ahead."

"That'd be about right. We were diggin' just up ahead where the tunnel branches off to the right. Jillian's got lanterns, but she's also got—"

Suddenly, a figure pounced from the spot where the dim light was coming from and leapt into the tunnel facing Clint. There wasn't much to see besides a human-shaped shadow, but its posture and the way it held its hands told Clint that there was a gun being pointed directly at him.

Clint reflexively brought his Colt around, but hesitated to fire. "Jillian," he called out, "if that's you, don't shoot. I've got your father with me."

At first, Clint could hear the distinct sound of a hammer being clicked into position. Then, a trembling voice drifted down the tunnel. "I-Is that you, Clint?"

"It's me all right. Come on over here and help me bring Eldon into the light."

The figure came running toward him. When it got halfway down the tunnel, Clint could see the shape of Jillian's body.

She had her hands outstretched and was carrying a small lantern in one hand. The light was turned down to almost nothing, but it was enough to let Clint see her beautiful, concerned face.

"You're a sight for sore eyes," Clint said as she looped Eldon's other arm over her neck and took some of the old man's weight upon herself.

"Oh my god, Father, are you hurt?"

Even though it was obviously a painful effort to draw in a breath, Eldon did his best not to show how much it hurt. His legs moved steadily but weakly beneath him once he could see the light up ahead. "It's not as bad as it looks, darlin'."

They made it to the split in the tunnel and turned right. There, they came upon a spot where several lanterns had been set up. A couple of torches had been fastened to the wall and all of Eldon's tools lay strewn about the floor. Clint and Jillian set Eldon gently down so he could lay with his back propped up against one wall.

For the first time, Clint was able to see where the old man had been shot. There was a dark, wet spot on his chest and most of the front of his shirt was soaked through with blood. "I don't know, Eldon," Clint said. "It looks pretty bad."

Eldon grit his teeth and tried to adjust how he was sitting. Even that little bit of effort brought a shudder to his body. His hands clawed at the stone floor as intense pain ravaged him right down to the core. "I can . . . feel it. The bullet. It's still inside."

Gently, Clint looked at Eldon's back. "You're right. There's no exit wound. I'm no doctor, but as long as you're breathing, you've got a chance." Moving in front of him to look Eldon straight in the eyes, Clint said, "You hear me? Hang on and I'll get you out of here."

The old man's eyes clenched shut for a second as he took a breath. When he opened them, the strength that had been keeping him going shone through and he nodded. "I ain't going nowhere. Jus' give me a gun and I'll hold the fort."

"I'll take care of Hardam. You just worry about—" Just then, something caught Clint's attention. It was something that glinted at him from the corner of his eye. At first, he thought it was a reflection off of one of the metal tools laying nearby, but when he turned, there was nothing on the ground. The wall, however, was another story.

Clint had heard miners refer to veins of gold or silver, but had always thought it to be an expression. In the space of a second, he'd been shown what those men had truly meant. He could see why they struggled their whole lives digging in dangerous tunnels and sifting through dirt at the bottom of rivers.

They were looking for something like this.

Running along the base of the wall as though it had been painted there was a fat streak of glittering yellow that caught the light from the lantern and broke it into a million tiny stars all down the length of the tunnel. On the floor, also, there were chunks of the stuff as big as Clint's fist. The vein ran behind Eldon's back and split off into smaller, finger-like branches that went up into the ceiling and down into the floor.

"Jillian," Clint said softly. "Maybe you'd better give him a gun."

She reached down to one of the piles of tools and pulled out what looked like a piece of short timber. Then, once it came free of the picks and shovels, the object could be seen for what it was: a shotgun that had not only a sawed-off barrel, but a stock that had been chipped away until it wasn't much more than a chunk of battered wood. Jillian gave the shoddy-looking weapon to Eldon, who took it and set it across his lap.

After finding a canteen and setting it within Eldon's reach, Clint pulled Jillian aside. "He won't be able to hold on much longer," he told her. "And Hardam won't wait too long himself before coming after us. Do you know any other way for us to circle around back to the entrance besides the tunnel we just came out of?"

She thought for a few seconds and nodded. "This tunnel we're in isn't a part of the regular mine, but it connects with a lot of the shafts. The man who sold it to us never found this tunnel. That's why he sold it to us."

"So who else knows about it?"

"As far as I know . . . nobody."

"Not unless Hardam decides to follow after us, that is." Looking down the other end of the roughly formed passage, Clint asked, "Where does this lead?"

"I've only been down there once. The gold only stretches for another twenty feet or so, so I never went much farther than that."

"Damn," Clint hissed. "I need to know if there's some way to circle around and cut Hardam off, but we don't have any time to explore."

Jillian looked at Clint with a puzzled expression. "Explore? Why would you have to explore?"

She put her hand on his chest, running it over his muscles and eventually beneath his jacket. Just when Clint was about to pull away, she pulled her hand free and held something in front of him.

"Did you forget about this?" she asked, holding the map he'd taken from Eldon.

At that moment, Clint was grateful for the darkness so his embarrassment didn't have to be so obvious. He took the map from her and walked back closer to the lanterns, where he unfolded it and quickly studied Eldon's sketches. Although crude, the drawings were more than enough to give Clint something to work with.

Suddenly, he spotted a notation that Eldon had made. It wasn't much more than a single, scribbled line, but it showed Clint exactly what he had to do next.

"What is it?" Jillian asked after she noticed the expression on Clint's face. "What did you find?"

"It could just be the second mother lode of the day."

FORTY-ONE

Hardam listened to Clint and the old man escape through the tunnel branching off from the main shaft. Once the footsteps were far enough away, he looked for himself and saw nothing but blackness. He pounded his fist in frustration and swore into the shadows before turning to check and see how Jervis was doing.

The gunman stood in the entrance to the mine, clutching his right shoulder. Trickles of red seeped out from between his fingers.

"You all right?" Hardam asked.

Grunting more in frustration than pain, Jervis moved his hand away so he could get a look at his shoulder. "It's just a scratch. Adams will get a hell of a lot more than this when I catch up to him." Jervis moved over next to Hardam and peered into the large crack in the wall. He held his lantern inside and surveyed the floor and ceiling. "How far in do you think this goes?"

"How the hell should I know?"

"I'll tell the others to get in here and we'll go after them."

"No," Hardam said. "If this is just a big dead end, Adams will have to come around to us. And if it leads somewhere, we know how to find them. What we need to do is make our preparations and get this over with. The longer we wait, the more time Adams has to find a way out."

171

"What preparations did you have in mind?"

"Come on. I'll show you."

Welles and the third man Jervis had brought along were already on their way up the cliff face when Hardam rode down on horseback. All three of them accompanied the wagon all the way to the front of the mine. Dismounting, Welles took a look around at the body laying near the entrance.

"We heard the shooting," Welles said. "What happened?"

Hardam and the other gunman were busy unloading the wagon, setting more sticks of dynamite carefully onto the ground. "Adams gave us a fight, but he's on the run now."

"Where's Bosner?"

"Dead."

That single word hit Welles like a jab to his face. Although he hadn't been good friends with Bosner, he'd known the man for some time. Hearing Hardam dismiss the man's life so easily was what struck Welles the most. It showed just where his boss's priorities were.

"Don't just stand there looking like a slack-jawed fool," Hardam snapped. "Make yourself useful and help us."

"What about Jervis? Did Adams—"

"He's inside waiting for Adams and the old man to show their faces again. When they do, we'll blow them off for what they done to Bosner and Anderson."

Welles looked down at the body next to the wagon. It was one of Rattler's men, just like the other man helping to unload the wagon. He didn't even know their names, but one of them was dead because of this whole thing. Knowing better than to ask Hardam anything else, Welles stepped in line and helped unload the explosives.

Before long, most of the dynamite was strewn about in small piles arranged near the entrance to the mine. Hardam was still fussing with some of the fuses, connecting most of the dynamite to a single detonator while making a few smaller individual packs.

"So this is the big plan, huh?" Welles said. "Just blow the whole thing up. What about all the gold that was supposed to be inside? What about all the money you promised us?"

One second, Hardam was occupied with his tasks and in the next, he was on his feet and storming toward Welles with a handful of dynamite clutched in a trembling fist.

"Question me again, you useless son of a bitch!" Hardam raged. "Go ahead, because I'm curious to see just how much of this stuff I can jam down your fucking throat."

Everyone stopped what they were doing.

Rattler's man was crouched down at the opposite side of the entrance setting up a few of the bombs Hardam had put together. Welles simply stared into Hardam's wild eyes, trying to keep his composure while also trying not to let on that he was too scared to move. He'd never seen Hardam like this. Plenty of times, the man had been intent on whatever he was after. That was how he got to be where he was. But in all his years with the small band of outlaws, Welles would never had said that Hardam was crazy.

Not until now, anyway.

After a few moments passed in silence, Hardam lowered the explosives he'd been holding and backed off just a bit. "Adams ran to get away from us. He might have taken a few of us with him, but he's hurt and on the run. All we have to do is wait him out and he'll have no choice but to come right to us."

"Then what are the explosives for?" Welles asked.

"Once we got what we want, we take out the entrance to the mines to cover our asses. Do you know who else the old man told about this place? Do you know if he wrote it somewhere or has anything set up to stake his claim? Do you know any of that?"

"He never said—"

"That's right. Well it won't matter a whole lot who he told or what he did if there ain't no mine anymore. With this place gone, we can have our gold, bury our competition and get away leaving behind nothing but a pile of rocks to mark all of our graves."

Once again, Welles felt a blow from Hardam's words that knocked him back worse than any punch he'd ever taken. "What *graves*?" he asked.

Hardam smiled and nodded slowly. Turning toward the

mine entrance, he swept his hands to indicate the entire setup he'd created. "Nobody comes away from this. Not old man Greary, not his daughter, not Clint Adams and not even us. Everyone in town knows about what we been doing to that old miner. With this much money at stake, they'll either be out to take it away from us or put the law onto our tails. Once we get enough of that gold, we blast this place sky-high and all anyone'll find is a smoking heap. Why bother digging for bodies when it's plain to see there ain't no survivors. And you know who'll come looking for us then?"

Welles slowly looked back and forth as Hardam's words sank in. "Nobody."

"That's right. We all get our cake and eat it too." Hardam stepped back like a proud artist showing off his masterpiece. "Who's crazy now?"

FORTY-TWO

Hardam strode into the mine as though he was its rightful owner. Behind him, Welles put the last touches on the large detonator box, which would seal up the mine for the better part of the next century.

Jervis and both of his remaining partners stood guard next to the opening to the fissure, which had since been cleared of most of the rocks that had been blocking its entrance. All three men were looking excitedly into the passage, waving for Hardam to come closer.

"What is it?" Hardam asked as he stepped up next to Jervis. "You look like you can barely hold yer water."

"Just listen," Jervis said in a whisper.

Hardam did and only had to wait a second or two before he heard footsteps coming from deep within the passage. Leaning back, he wore a proud smile on his face. "I told you he'd have to come back this way. Now you men take cover and get ready. As soon as you can see him, let me know and I'll take care of the rest."

Hardam watched as Jervis and the others carried out his orders. Confident in himself after watching Adams fight on several occasions, Hardam was certain he'd come up with the best way to kill the man. Just cut off his escape route and overpower him. Adams might get through some or all of Rattler's men, but that didn't matter much since they were just there as a shield.

It was a simple enough plan, but brilliance was always mired in simplicity. Moving back, Hardam took hold of one of the smaller sticks of dynamite and removed the top from a nearby lantern. Once Adams was close enough, the passage would be blown and Adams would either be trapped or dead. After that, it was just a matter of picking up his gold.

Hardam was close enough to the passage that he could hear Adams coming. Just another few seconds and . . .

"What the hell?" Jervis grunted as he nudged the man standing next to him.

Suddenly, both men turned to look toward the curve in the mine shaft. The man next to Jervis went for his gun, only to be knocked off his feet by a shot that echoed through the enclosed space like a clap of thunder. The single bullet tore a hole clean through the man's chest and sparked against the wall as it came out of his back.

Jervis already had his pistol out and started bringing it up to aim at where that shot had come from. Because of his wound, however, he took a split-second too long, which was all the time needed for a second shot to blast through the musty air to carve a fresh tunnel through the gunman's skull.

Hardam reeled back from the passage's entrance, the entire front of his shirt covered in the blood of his men. Those two were supposed to have been good enough to keep Adams busy, but they'd died before Hardam could even get so much as another glimpse of the Gunsmith. As much as he wanted to do something, he was torn as to which way to go. Although the footsteps in the passage were still getting closer, he knew the shots had actually come from deeper within the mine itself.

"Welles," he screamed over his shoulder. "Get in here!"

A figure emerged from the darkness. Hardam could see it now. It came from the depths of the mine, trailing a wisp of smoke in its wake. Another figure could be seen inside the passage, walking hunched over inside the tight confines of the natural crevice.

Welles came running into the mine, his gun drawn. Next

to him, Rattler's last hired gun stood quickly surveying the scene. His eyes landed on Jervis and stayed there, a stunned look drifting onto his face.

"It's all over," Clint shouted as he stepped into the dim light given off by Hardam's lanterns. He emerged from the mine tunnel and stood where the passage curved toward the entrance. The fissure lay ahead of him, still marked by Eldon's blood.

"Time for you to stop hiding behind your men and face me for yourself," Clint said. There was no challenge in his voice, or even a threat. What he said was a simple fact. Nothing more.

Hardam looked between Clint, the bodies on the ground, and the remaining two men standing behind him. The dynamite trembled in his hand as his mind tried to wrap around how his plan could have been countered so easily. "Where did you come from?" he asked while staring at the large crack in the wall. "I saw you go in there. I waited this whole time . . ."

"There was no way for you to know," Clint stated. "Because I was the only one who had this." Raising his left hand, he held up the folded map Eldon had drawn. "That crack actually leads somewhere. And that somewhere circles back around to join up with the mine farther down." Clint stuffed the map back into his pocket and stared across at Hardam. "Bet you didn't know that."

"So what now?" Hardam asked.

"That's up to you. Drop that detonator and clear all of this dynamite out of here would be a good start. After that, you'll have to come with me so I can hand you over to the law."

"I don't think so." Pointing at Clint with the dynamite in his hand, Hardam said, "You're still outnumbered, Adams. So go ahead and shoot, because you can't hit all of us before we gun you down. And just to make sure . . ." Hardam lowered his hand so he could touch the end of the fuse to a nearby lantern's flame. The fuse sparked to life and hissed like an angry snake as Hardam brought his hand back up to show what he'd done. To the men standing behind him, he said, "Kill this son of a bitch."

The footsteps coming from the passage got louder and quicker as Hardam tossed the dynamite into it. The stick landed and spun on its side as the fuse sputtered closer to the blasting point. There was less than an inch to go when Jillian got to it and snuffed it out between thumb and fore-finger.

"It's all right, Clint," she shouted. "Finish it."

Clint stepped a little closer. He'd sent Jillian down the tunnel knowing that Hardam's men would be waiting there for him. He'd only asked her to provide a distraction and then jump for cover, but she'd wound up proving a lot more useful than he could've ever hoped.

Looking at Hardam, studying the positions of all the gun-men, Clint dropped his Colt back into its holster and kept his hand over its handle. "You heard the lady. Let's put an end to this."

The anger on Hardam's face boiled over to rage. His fin-gers shifted anxiously as he began stepping back away from the passage. "What are you waiting for?" he shouted over his shoulder. "I told you to *kill him*!"

Welles and Rattler's last remaining gunman stood behind Hardam as though they didn't know whether to draw or just walk away.

"There's only three of us left," Hardam said. "That means we each get a bigger share once Adams is dead. That's a full third share for each of us. Right now, we're equal partners."

Clint stood completely still, waiting to see if the other two would let greed or common sense get the better of them. His answer came in less than a second as both of the gunmen turned to face Clint and grabbed for their guns.

As soon as Hardam saw what was happening, he dropped and threw himself back toward the mine's entrance. He landed on his belly and began immediately scrambling for another one of the individual sticks of dynamite he'd pre-pared.

Rattler's man was first to clear leather.

Since he was far enough away and still in the shadows, Clint couldn't tell which one was going to shoot at him until he saw the glint of light off the barrel of the other man's weapon. Even before he was conscious of what he'd seen, Clint's body was already reacting to it, causing him to pluck the Colt from its place at his side, bring it up and fire off a single round from the hip.

For a moment, the gunman's body twitched and didn't move. Right as Clint was going to send another round his way, he saw the man drop straight down to his knees and then fall forward onto his face. His hand was still on the handle of his gun.

Clint could read the indecision on Welles's face. One moment Welles looked as though he was about to fire and then the next, he retreated another step toward the mine's entrance. More than anything else, he looked like he just wanted to leave.

"It's too late to go now," Clint said. "You've come too far to just run away."

Hardam looked as if he didn't know what the hell Clint was talking about. When he turned to look at Welles, he saw what the other man was doing, which ignited his rage to even bigger heights. "You cowardly son of a bitch. All this goid to split only two ways and you want to run away?"

"Can't spend nothin' if we're dead," Welles said quietly.

FORTY-THREE

Clint held his gun ready to fire on either one of the two remaining men. Welles was becoming more desperate with every passing second and Hardam was on the brink of just about anything. What he wasn't ready for was to see Hardam's expression go from wild fury to grim satisfaction.

"Kill Adams now," Hardam said while holding up a stick of dynamite and tearing the fuse in half, "or we all die together."

Clint heard the threat and started moving forward to get to Hardam before he lit the shortened fuse, but then he stopped short when he saw Welles turn toward him with gun in hand.

Everything happened so quickly, Clint was surprised he could see it all.

Within the space of a heartbeat, Welles looked to Clint and brought his gun up to fire. He shook his head almost as if to apologize for what he was about to do.

Hardam did the only thing he was good for when the shooting started, which was to do his best to get the hell out of the way. He rolled to the side, giving Clint a quick view of the dynamite in his hand. The fuse had somehow been lit and was already crackling toward the red bundle of explosives.

Seeing this, Clint's brain pumped a surge of adrenalin

though his body that launched his hand into a set of motions that flowed so quickly, they would have easily been missed by the naked eye.

First, he swung his hand up, took quick aim and fired off a shot toward Welles. Next, he dropped his hand a few inches, let out the breath he'd been holding and fired again, this time aiming for a spot no bigger than the tip of a candle, knowing that a miss would spell out certain doom for everyone in the immediate vicinity.

Both rounds found their mark. One slammed into Welles's chest and knocked him onto the floor with arms and legs spread at awkward angles. The second spun through the air, whipped over Hardam's shoulder, tore through a bit of flesh and bone and sparked off the ground after nipping off the part of the fuse that was a hair's length away from igniting the explosives.

Clint stood motionless for a second until he was certain that the dynamite wasn't about to go off. He then spun the Colt once and dropped it back into his holster.

Jillian waited at the mouth of the passage, which split off from the mine shaft, with her gun ready to defend Clint if she was needed. Ignoring the bodies strewn at her feet, she stepped out of the fissure and tried to hold her gun in shaking hands.

When he heard her moving, Clint turned and walked over to her. "Are you all right?" he asked.

"Yes," she said in a trembling voice. "Scared as hell, but I'll be ok."

"We need to get to Eldon before—"

"Nobod . . . nobody gets that gold," came a ragged voice from the front of the mine. "Unless it's me!"

At once, Clint and Jillian spun on their heels to see what was going on. They immediately spotted Hardam laying on the floor, gripping his dynamite in a hand that only had a thumb and part of a finger to grip with. Apparently, Clint's bullet had cut a bit more than just the fuse.

"I ain't goin' to jail," Hardam groaned. The pain washed through his voice like bile. His eyes were alight with pain and blood poured down from the stumps at the end of his hand. "And I ain't lettin' you get out of here with my money." Holding up the dynamite, he drew in a breath and struck a match with his good hand. "If you want to live, then get that gold and—"

Suddenly, Welles lunged up from the floor and grabbed hold of both of Hardam's wrists. Already, his skin had blanched to the color of fresh linen and was covered in a thin sweaty film. His eyes were glazed over, yet locked on their goal.

Clint had seen men like this before. Rather than lay back and let what little bit of life was in them drain away, they pulled it together and burned it at once. He figured Welles had about five more seconds before he dropped. When he spoke, Welles sounded like a cold wind blowing through dead trees.

"You . . . always . . . talked too much," he groaned. "Just once . . . I want you . . . to . . . back it . . . up . . ." And with that, he pushed Hardam's hands together, bringing the match closer and closer to the stick of dynamite.

Clint whipped around and launched himself toward the fissure, slamming his shoulder into Jillian's stomach and wrapping both arms tightly around her body. Although he might have knocked the wind out of her, he also knocked her off her feet and pushed her toward the gaping crack in the wall.

A few more steps, and they were in the rough passage, landing one on top of another as the initial heat from the blast scorched over Clint's back.

The explosion rocked the floor, walls and ceiling, causing dust and rocks to shower down upon them. When the fire came, it flashed through the tunnel and licked the edge of the fissure before moving on to burn itself out in the bigger spaces of the shaft itself.

More rocks dropped from overhead, but stopped just short of triggering a full cave-in. Once the other set of explosives started going off, however, the word *cave-in* wasn't nearly enough to describe the deafening sound of the mine's entrance collapsing in on itself.

After what seemed like an eternity, Clint rolled off of Jillian and dusted himself off.

"Are we still alive?" she asked weakly.

"If Hardam had been any better with explosives, we sure wouldn't be. Are you hurt?"

"I'm healthy enough to move, so let's just get my father and get out of this hole."

Clint wasn't about to argue with that. And he definitely wasn't about to go near the front of that mine.

FORTY-FOUR

Neither Clint or Jillian so much as looked back at the destruction Hardam had created. Even though it had sounded as though the cliff was coming down on top of them, the natural fissure they were in had sustained little or no damage. Besides being shaken up, the passage seemed to have survived the punishment dealt by the explosion.

They found Eldon equally shaken, but alive all the same.

"Well," he said as Clint helped him to his feet. "If we can't go out the way we came, how do you suppose we go home?"

"Don't try to test me," Clint warned. "I read your map well enough to find the second entrance to this place."

"Sure, but that's all the way at the other end of the mine. And we'll have to walk down . . ."

Clint listened to the old man bitch for the next several hours. At least it kept him awake and thinking about something besides the wound in his chest. Once they emerged back into the light, Clint found himself looking down upon a narrow path roughly a hundred feet over the larger entrance, which had been reduced to a pile of rocks and timber. It was tough going, but they managed to climb down.

Back at the wagon, Jillian was able to get to her medical supplies and bandage Eldon up good enough to make it back into town.

• • •

A week later, Clint and Jillian were on their way back to the cliff. This time, they took their time and made something of a vacation out of it. When they were in sight of the trail leading up the side, they climbed off their horses and went the rest of the way on foot.

"How's your father doing?" Clint asked, even though he'd seen Eldon not more than a day ago.

"He'll live. His mining days are over, but he'll make it. The doctor says the bullet was lodged in one of his ribs." She grimaced and shook her head as a chill went through her body. "It took him an hour to get the damn thing out of him, but it didn't get to anything vital."

"He's a tough old bird. I've seen men trying to be gunfighters reduced to tears after getting hit like that and he still managed to walk down the side of that thing," Clint said, pointing to the cliff. "He's really amazing."

Jillian stopped and took hold of Clint's shirt. Pressing her back against a section of the cliff that was covered with lush green vines, she pulled him in close and kissed him gently on the mouth. "If you don't mind, I'd like to think about something else besides my father right now."

Clint pretended to be more concerned with the trail ahead of him, looking toward it as though it was calling his name. "But . . . if we're gonna go back for some of that gold, we should probably get a move on. It'll be hard enough with just the two of us and—"

Her hand drifted over his stomach and settled on the bulge at his crotch. "I'd say it's just about hard enough." She kissed him hard on the mouth, her tongue slipping between his lips as her hand massaged him until he was fully erect. Writhing against the stone, she leaned her head back and smiled broadly. "It's like I can feel all the gold on my skin already, Clint. And when I think about all the danger we had to go through . . . all the excitement . . . it just makes me feel so glad to be alive. I want to celebrate that with you. Right here. Right now."

Clint forgot about everything else he was going to say or do. All that was on his mind was Jillian. Her skin, her body, her flesh called out to him and when he pulled off her clothes and slid his hands along her naked body, there was no turning back.

In seconds, they'd torn each other's clothes off and stood up against the cliff. She raised her leg and wrapped it around his waist as Clint's hand slid beneath her buttocks and held her up. With both hands, she stroked his penis and then guided it into her. As soon as he felt the warm wetness engulfing his shaft, Clint slid it all the way inside and held it there, savoring the moment for all it was worth.

Jillian dug her nails into Clint's shoulders and arched her back against the cliff. With her eyes clenched, she let out a passionate cry that was so loud it rolled through the trees and faded away into the distance. Every time he thrust into her, she grunted and bucked, surrendering every part of her to the moment.

Clint grabbed her by the hips and pound into her once more before pulling out and kissing her on the neck. He worked his lips farther down along her neck and then licked her breasts, focusing especially on the hard, pink little nipples. All the while, his hands roamed over her sides and between her legs, rubbing here and there as her entire body writhed in ecstasy.

Soon, his tongue was going lower until Clint dropped to his knees and started placing gentle kisses along the top of the dark patch of hair between her thighs. Jillian ran her fingers through his hair and when he licked the pink lips of her vagina, she thrust her hips forward and let out another loud moan.

Resting one thigh on Clint's shoulder, Jillian raised one arm over her head and let a satisfied grin drift across her face as she leaned back and enjoyed the movement of Clint's lips and tongue between her legs. It wasn't long before jolts of pleasure began lancing through her body, causing her to moan louder and louder until the orgasm exploded from inside of her.

She then stepped back and playfully shoved Clint onto his back with one foot on his chest. The moment he landed, she was on top of him, straddling his hips and settling over his erect shaft. Jillian spread her legs and squatted down, impaling herself on his cock and then lowering down until he was all the way inside of her.

Looking up at her, enjoying the way she arched her back as she bounced slowly up and down on top of him, Clint couldn't think of anything else but the beautiful curves of Jillian's body and the way the sunlight danced within her flowing hair.

It was an hour or so before Clint and Jillian were dressed and ready to continue up to the smaller entrance leading down to the mine. On the way, they passed the ruins of the main entrance.

"Why do you think we made it?" Jillian asked quietly as she stared down at the burnt rubble.

"My guess is that the natural passage had been there a lot longer than the mine, so it was a hell of a lot sturdier. Also, Hardam didn't put enough explosives in the right places to—"

"That's not what I meant. I mean, how come we survived at all? Father got shot, I could've been shot or blown up when I was coming down that passage and you could've been dead more times than I care to think about."

Clint shrugged and wrapped his arms around her. "All I can say is that Hardam was out to kill and we were just trying to live. In the end, we all got what we wanted."

They made the rest of the climb in contented silence. Unfortunately, on the way down, there was no time for another celebration since it was all they could do to keep from falling off the side while carrying so much gold.

Watch for

OUTLAW LUCK

243rd novel in the exciting GUNSMITH series
from Jove

Coming in March!